PURE

TRENTON SECURITY BOOK 4

J.M. DABNEY

HOSTILE WHISPERS PRESS, LLC

Copyright © 2019 by J.M. Dabney

Hostile Whispers Press, LLC

ISBN: 978-1-947184-32-9

Cover by: Reese Dante

Edits by: AlternativEdits (Laura McNellis)

Proof Edit by: Stephanie Carrano

REMEMBER:

This book is a work of fiction. All characters, places, and events are from the author's imagination and should not be confused with fact. Any resemblance to persons, living or dead, events or places, is purely coincidental.

PLEASE BE ADVISED:

This book contains material that is only suitable for mature readers. It may contain scenes of a sexual nature and/or violence.

For my readers who make all my books possible.

Special thanks to the people who keep me sane, Tracey, Steph, Meredith and Jenn, Erica, who keep me writing through the doubt and make my books better.

AUTHOR NOTE

This book contains a scene of rape, while it's not done it extreme detail it was relevant to the story. If you have any issues with these scenes please skip the Prologue where the mentioned scene takes place.

PROLOGUE

ATLANTA, GEORGIA 2004

$\mathscr{N}$icolas Warner flinched as the nurse cleaned the cut on his lip as he clutched the warmed blanket tighter around himself. He'd fought back the tears for the last hour and refused to make eye contact with the bored-looking uniform cop in the corner. They'd found a shirt that fit him after they'd sent him to x-ray his ribs.

Twelve hours ago, he'd nearly bounced with excitement about his first date with a boy. His mom had kissed his cheek with a smile and told him to have fun. As always, she'd reminded him in her cautious way to be safe. He'd known forever he wasn't like everyone else. When he was ten, he'd told his mom he was going to marry the Prince in his favorite bedtime story.

He'd thought he was too old for them, pretended to hate it, but his mom worked so many hours that it was their special time. They'd curl up in her double bed and read. She'd told him the perfect Prince to look for. That the one perfect for him would wait. His mom said when it was right that he'd find someone to love him and show him the respect and care.

He was big and soft around the middle, and no one had looked at him until the popular boy in his high school asked him to come and hang out. Said it would just be the two of them. The guy smiled, and for the first time, he felt that odd feeling in his stomach, turned shy, and the guy had lifted his hand. When the other boy had tucked his fingers under his chin, he hadn't been able to help but let his smile show.

Then it had all gone to hell.

"Come on, Nicky, everyone else is doing it."

"No, we talked about this."

He was waiting for love. He was only fifteen, and he wasn't ready to take that step for anyone, especially the first time they hung out. There wasn't any shame in holding out for someone who wanted more than to just get off and use him as a tool to do so. He flinched at the painful grip on his crotch. He jumped back, but the guy just kept coming.

"I said no. I want to go home." He turned and realized his mistake when strong arms circled him from behind.

The fear choked him as he tried to free his arms, but he grunted as he was pushed over the tailgate of the guy's truck. His baggy jeans were ripped over his backside, and he screamed as fingers were shoved inside. He cried and begged—kicked as the guy told him just to relax that he'd like it. The pressure and pain disappeared, but his terror escalated as he heard the jingle of a belt buckle.

He fought against the hand that was pressing into the center of his back. He clawed at the rusted metal of the truck bed.

Naked hips and a thick erection pressed to him, and the blunt tip ripped through the tightness of his hole. The agony caused nausea to build. He cried, and his nails ripped when they caught on a jagged spot of flaky metal. The burn caused him to gag, and he choked as his dinner came up. He fought for breath as the boy raped him.

"What the fuck is going on here," a stranger's voice screamed from the darkness.

He didn't hesitate to use the distraction to his advantage, and as he held his pants, his backside still bared, he ran into the night. No destination. He didn't even know where he was. All he knew was he needed to escape. Tears and snot streaked his face. His sobs were loud, and he couldn't stop running. He couldn't get far enough away.

He barely choked back another sob as his mom pushed aside the curtain. He ignored his aching ribs and just buried his face in her throat. She was in her nurse's uniform. His feet hit the floor, and he ran into her arms.

"Nick, are you okay?"

"Can we talk about this in front of your mother?"

He only nodded and tried to ignore them, telling his mother what happened. Shame and disgust nearly took him out at the knees. His tiny mother braced him as if she'd never let him fall. He didn't want to hear the word. Didn't want to name it. If he didn't talk about it, then it wouldn't exist. That his stupidity hadn't made him a victim—he cried harder and only listened to his mother's soothing tone.

"Honey, we're alone, come on, sit up on the gurney."

He didn't want to obey. He didn't want to see her disappointment.

"Nicolas Warner, you look at me right now."

He lifted his chin from his chest and looked at his mother.

"You listen to me. This is not your fault. Don't let this color your dreams."

All he wanted to do was disappear, and her strong hands holding his face forced him to meet her gaze.

"We're going to go home. You'll get in a hot bath, and then you'll talk it out. Don't let this fester."

He agreed with her, just a simple nod to appease her, and he waited there dying a bit more inside as he waited for his discharge papers. There was no Prince for him. No happily ever after. He'd never be weak again. No man would ever hold him down and take. He wasn't the person he'd been when he left his house, and he never would be again. He could already feel it—they'd stolen a piece of him, and he'd never get it back—no matter how much time or healing.

IT WAS JUST STITCHES

*A*n angry, pissed off biker in leathers glared at him from the other side of the exam room. Powerful arms corded with muscle and veined forearms were crossed over a chest with rounded pectorals pushing at black cotton. Raul Martinez snarled and one thick dark brow bisected with a scar was arched and dared him to complain.

He tried to hold the angry stare, but the blood still flowing into his eye ruined the effect. It probably looked like he was winking at the man. Which he would never do. He didn't flirt, especially not with men like Raul.

It was just stitches that he could've handled himself, but Raul had decided he was Pure's keeper. Six months ago, Raul had come to work for Trenton Security full-time, and it had been hell. They fought enough when Raul took the occasional bounty from Linus, but the man in the office every day pushed all Pure's buttons.

"You don't have to stay."

"Shut up. I ain't going anywhere. You'll fucking sneak out."

Pure was thirty, and he'd taken care of himself for a long time.

He didn't need some overbearing brute trying to boss him around. He laid his head back and closed his eyes.

"Don't dare go to sleep."

"Go away!"

He was getting tired of Raul ordering him around like he...owned him. The man wasn't his boyfriend or even his friend. He wouldn't even let a boyfriend boss him around. Not that he'd ever had one, because the few dates he'd had didn't call for a second when they found out he didn't have sex. He refused to have a man use him as a masturbatory tool because his pleasure and care wasn't worth their effort.

It wasn't like he didn't want to, he just wanted to wait for the right guy. One who'd stick around. His dad hadn't. The man had spouted all the right words, used love as a weapon to get what he wanted. Pure's mother had been left pregnant and alone a few days before her eighteenth birthday. She'd found herself homeless and working as a waitress, no high school diploma, and living in a falling down trailer. Pure had done right by her. She had everything she'd ever dreamed, and he worked hard so she didn't have to. Even though she went to nursing school, he hadn't changed his habit of sending her the extra he earned or showing up with special gifts.

He still felt Raul staring at him, and it pissed him off. "I said, go away."

"Not happening."

"Hey, Pure, back to see me again?"

He lifted his head to see the usual ER doctor breeze in. The man was handsome and probably about his age. His visits normally correlated with this doctor's. His name was Carlton, and the man had asked him out for coffee. He'd politely declined, and it hadn't been brought up again.

"Not by choice."

"I see that," Carl said with a friendly smile. The man turned to where Raul stood. "Sir, will you leave us so I can—"

"Like that, wouldn't you, pretty boy?" Raul started to push away from the wall.

No one might think he paid much attention to the dangerous man other than when they were fighting, but that wasn't true, he knew what the man was getting ready to do. "Raul!"

Raul pivoted with the grace of a trained warrior and glared at him. "What?"

"Quit being an asshole."

"He wants—"

"Shut up. He wants to know if he should call the cops in case I'm being abused."

"I would never fucking put my hands on you, Pure. What the fuck?"

It was odd to see Raul looking offended and slightly hurt. They fought, a lot, but he never once thought Raul would ever hit him. The man seemed obsessively protective of him—which was weird since he was at least three inches taller and about fifty pounds heavier than Raul. Raul was a fighter. Brutal when it came to his work. And, yes, the man was an asshole, but he wasn't bad when Raul wasn't ordering him around.

"It's standard procedure when someone has as many visits as Pure does, and you always seem to be the one with him. I'm aware of his profession, but that doesn't erase the chance of domestic abuse. Let's check you out."

Raul was strangely quiet. The man was eerily silent on most days—an observer—and Raul didn't miss a thing. Except when Raul had anger rolling off him in waves, Pure knew the man was ready to strike. They'd spent several years anticipating their moods and moves, so they worked as a perfectly synchronized team.

"I don't have a concussion. I'm not nauseous, my head does hurt but nothing out of the ordinary when you headbutt a wall." He heard Raul's deep growl and knew what was coming. He didn't need another lecture. "Raul, don't start."

"Why don't you let me be the judge if you have a concussion or not?"

"Yes, sir," Pure grumbled.

If Carl hadn't been prodding the cut, he would've jerked his head to see what Raul was steaming about. He winced as Carl pushed a little too hard and pain exploded in his head. Calloused fingertips stroked along his forearm and then thick fingers pushed between his. He flinched more from the strangeness of Raul holding his hand than the pain.

Raul went out of his way to avoid contact with him. Occasionally, Raul would place a hand on his back or shoulder as they entered a building to do a take-down or when he acted as Sniper and Raul took the job as his spotter.

"You're going to need stitches and someone to watch you at least overnight. Your mom?"

"No, I bought her a two-week cruise. They've been short-staffed in the emergency room, and she had to pull a lot of doubles. She deserved to escape for a bit."

"I bet Jenn loved that."

When he got nervous, he talked, and he'd told Carl about his mom over coffee while he'd waited to take Little home one night.

"She's having a blast. Even said she shared dinner with a gentleman she met."

"Love in the air?"

"Oh, man, I hope not."

"You're going to feel some pinches and stinging while I numb the cut. Why do you hope not?"

"I don't know. It'll be weird."

The conversation continued through Carl numbing the cut and then carefully stitching. Raul didn't release his hand, and he even felt the odd caress to the inside of his wrist. It was comforting but disconcerting at the same time. He'd avoided physical contact with Raul; touching led him to think of things he didn't allow himself. Raul was good at making his mind wander to erotic situations, and some were embarrassing. He hoped no one ever stumbled across his collection of bookmarked porn videos.

He mentally shook off the thoughts that his brain was veering toward, and as he opened his eyes, Raul stepped away.

"So who's going—"

"I'll stay with him," Raul barked out before he had a chance to answer.

"I can take care of myself."

He pouted as Raul and Carl spoke, pretty much ignoring his protests. He didn't want Raul in his house. It was his sanctuary. The place he escaped from work. It didn't seem he had much choice in the matter though. The men kept talking about what to look for, but the Trenton team spent a lot of time in hospitals, and they all had medic training. He hated the hospital. It brought back too many memories. He'd spent most of his life trying to pretend that the incident hadn't happened.

Finally, Carl placed a bandage over the stitches. He rolled to a sitting position, and Raul excused himself for a minute. He looked down at his bloody, torn shirt, and wished he'd had a change of clothes. His go-bag was in Raul's truck, and he didn't get a chance to ask Raul to grab him a t-shirt.

"Pure, here." Raul pushed the curtain aside and handed him a t-shirt. "I'll wait outside while you get dressed and then we'll get you home."

"Thanks," he said.

He focused on Raul's retreating back and then got dressed as a nurse knocked. He signed the discharge papers and got the packet, along with instructions, and a reminder to catch up with his regular doctor to remove the stitches. He'd just have Little do it like he'd always done.

On the way home, he told himself to act natural and try to figure out a way to get Raul to drop him off, then just leave.

WASN'T THIS COZY?

*R*aul hovered beside the door as Pure moved around the house. The open floor plan let him see the dining room and kitchen, along with the living room. The place looked cozy and warm—the type of house you saw in magazines with families sitting around the fire.

He went back to observing Pure. The man was gorgeous and innocent, and he'd tried to ignore his attraction to Pure. The first time he'd met Pure, the man was decked out in tactical gear with his sniper rifle. His cock had instantly gone hard. He wasn't a eunuch. He'd gotten turned on by plenty of men in his life, but that had been the only time he had hardened just looking at someone.

The man was perfect from his brown hair to his size thirteen tactical boots. Pure was huge; six and a half feet, a good two hundred and sixty pounds, his muscles weren't hard or sleek. His —and yes Pure was his—man was bulky and soft. The curve of Pure's belly called for him to nuzzle. He couldn't claim his boy, but that didn't mean in his mind that his partner didn't belong to him.

"You can come in," Pure said without looking up from a stack of mail he was going through. "Hungry?"

"Nah, I'm good."

"It's too late to cook, but I have some leftovers."

Pure was nervous about him being there, so he figured letting the man feed him would be a good distraction. He knew they weren't best friends and probably never would be. With his background, relationships were a no-go, and Nicolas Warner screamed commitment. Who else would hold on to their virginity for thirty years? Pure would be like touching the sun. Someone who would wash away his sins or at least help him forget them. He couldn't allow himself to get burned.

Once he had Pure, he wouldn't let go, and that would turn into his biggest sin of all.

"Okay, what ya got?" he asked as he headed for the kitchen area.

When he walked in, he found Pure already bent over and looking in the fridge. Black fabric molded to the most spank-worthy ass he'd ever had the good fortune to see. Holy fuck, but was that ass deserving of a brutal pounding. That thought right there made him unworthy of Pure. He was not in any way, shape, or form the person to be someone's first anything, especially not fuck.

"Fried chicken, roasted brussel sprouts, and mashed sweet potatoes."

"You made that for just you?" He had a moment of jealousy thinking Pure was cooking for someone else.

"Yeah, we eat a lot of take-out, so when I'm home, I like to cook. Mom made me self-sufficient."

"Ain't a bad thing."

"If you don't like any of that, I can cook something else."

"Sounds perfect. I was just going to hit the fast-food drive-thru. Thanks." The word sounded foreign coming from his mouth. He didn't thank anyone because he never asked for anything. His parents worked their asses off to make sure he could take care of himself. His dad was a cop, and his mom was a nurse, and he'd done everything possible to make raising him hell.

"You're welcome."

Pure went about gathering everything and setting it on the small island, then turning to heat the oven. It was so domestic and shit, then a thought struck him. "Brownies."

Pure spared him one glance. "Brownies?"

"Where did you get the brownies you brought in last week? I asked Ben over at Decadence, and he had no idea."

"Oh, I made those. I think I have another—" Pure's voice trailed off as he opened another cabinet and pulled down a gallon-sized bag. "These?" Pure laid them on the island in front of him and went back to reheating dinner.

"Yeah, those were fucking amazing. So you cook and bake?"

He'd always wanted to ask Pure about himself, learn every detail, but he'd refrained from doing so. Maybe it overwhelmed his curiosity since he was about to spend the night to watch over Pure.

"Mom is a chocoholic. While she was working in the evenings, I'd make her brownies and cakes, whatever she mentioned she was craving. So, when she got home, she'd have something. I spent most of my chore money on learning to bake her the things she liked."

Could the man get any fucking sweeter? Pure couldn't be real. "Why's that?"

"She gave up a lot for me. The least I could do is make her a batch of cookies."

"What about your dad?"

"High school quarterback, the college star, then professional, but that's all I know. He went off to college and left Mom behind, pregnant."

"Didn't he help out? If he reached the professional level, then the man could afford—"

"He denied it, and, well, Mom was too embarrassed to come forward. Her family was fundamentally religious and disowned her. Mom just wanted to go on with her life and try to forget."

He looked around and noticed a picture on the fridge door. Pure with a tiny woman leaned against his side. Her head didn't even meet his armpit. That woman pushed out Pure. That shit boggled the mind.

"Is this her?" He walked around the island and pulled the picture from under the magnet.

"The day I left for bootcamp."

"Marine?" He'd known Pure was a sniper in the military, but he hadn't known which branch.

"Yeah. Mom couldn't afford college, and they'd pay."

"Why are you working as a bounty hunter slash sniper at Trenton, college boy?"

"Didn't go. I was out of the Marines by twenty-one, spent a year on the Atlanta PD S.W.A.T. team, and Linus recruited me to work for him. I got the chance to move home."

"Not all there is to it, I'm sure."

"Some guy on my team didn't like the word no, I loosened his teeth and broke his jaw."

"Good for you."

"Thanks. My commanding officer didn't see it that way." Pure opened the oven and slid in a baking sheet with their dinner on it, then straightened.

The idea of someone else putting their hands on Pure enraged him. Hell, he didn't even like other men standing near Pure. He needed to get over this obsession, or he was going to have to move on. It was easier to ignore when he was only a freelancer, getting the occasional call from Linus. For six months he'd been in the office full-time and living in Powers.

"Pure, man, you home, please be fucking home!"

He spun on his heels. He'd locked the damn door behind him, and suddenly Little was on his knees in front of Pure.

"Poe won't talk to me, ya gotta talk to him."

Poe was Little's pretty, little husband. They fought constantly, and it was actually cute to watch the tiny, chunky man take on a behemoth like Little. Little caved instantly.

"What did you do now?"

Little threw his arms around Pure's thighs and hung on tight. He wasn't liking Little touching Pure, but he had no right to say anything.

"He fell on my dick."

Pure groaned and threw his head back, then went back to glaring down at Little. "The last time Poe fell on your dick was when he woke up to pink hair, and you failed to tell him as he's panicking that it was temporary color. Or when Poe woke up, and you told him he was going to marry you. Or…"

"I get it, man, I do, but he's so sexy when he's mad, and I gotta have my man on my dick. Ya gotta call him, man. He always listens to you."

"Fine." Pure sighed and pulled out his phone.

"You made food?" Little surged to his feet and rushed to the oven. The man opened it and started picking things off the pan.

"Help yourselves."

He watched Pure roll his eyes and pulled his phone out of his pocket.

"Speaker," Little yelled with a mouth full of food.

"Yes, I'll put it on speaker."

"What the fuck is going on here?" he demanded.

"Poe only listens to Pure when he's mad at me."

"Are you sixteen? Take care of your own shit."

"I can't," Little loudly whined, and he looked more like a kid than a badass in his thirties.

"Pure, I don't want to talk about it." Poe's voice filled the kitchen.

"Poe, tell me what Little did this time. If you talk it out, then you can get his oversized ass out of my house. He ate everything I had last time. How do you afford him?"

"It's not easy. It's a full-time job just to keep him in groceries. His paycheck barely covers his energy drinks!"

"Hey, I make—"

"I'm not talking to you."

Poe yelled, and he even flinched at the high-pitched tone. Poe was a bit high-strung. The couple was weird, and they deserved each other—who else would put up with Little's shit except someone as crazy as him?

"Fuck, just tell me what he did."

Pure was getting tired, and the big man was starting to look worse for wear. The man needed to eat and go to bed and not deal with acting as a marriage counselor.

"He bought me presents."

"Do I even want to ask?"

"It's a hairless cat who hates me, and a huge iguana I'm sure is looking at the cat as a snack. I can't deal with that. What if the dragon eats the kitten and then I'm devastated by the guilt? This is too much pressure. This is why I vetoed kids. What if I had broken one? Now I'm going to watch the dragon devour the cat, and that's going to be forever burned into my brain. Little knows this. He does this to torture me."

Raul was pretty sure that the entire statement was made in one breath. He didn't know whether to laugh or run as far away from the insanity as he could get. He hadn't realized the full extent of Trenton and Crew craziness until he was witnessing it as a permanent member of the team.

"Harvey was only making friends with Twinkie!"

"See, he named the cat after a snack and Harvey is take…oh my fake Jesus, he's licking the cat again. He'll probably ask me for salt so the stringy little shit tastes decent. Did I mention I lost Harvey already or that I had to rescue Twinkie from sudden death after finding the hideous creature licking energy drink cans on Little's cesspool of a desk?"

"I told you Harvey might have some interspecies fetish, it's nothing," Little growled.

"Now I have to worry about dragons that look like cats when Harvey decides to put on some slow jams and light some—"

"Do you and Little live to torture me?" Pure demanded.

"I'm the normal one, Pure. Little is best friends with Lily. There is no amount of therapy to correct that! And let me tell you I've tried. I can't even sleep around him. He covered me in glitter and shined the spotlight on me so he could watch it reflect onto the ceiling! Six months and I'm ready—"

"Poe."

Oh shit, Little had a bit of separation anxiety leftover from when he was a kid, and his abandonment issues were legendary. Little's sad tone even made him feel bad for the guy.

"Oh shit, baby, I'm sorry. I didn't mean it. I promise. I love you. You know that."

"I want to come home."

One fucking tear and he was out of there, concussed Pure or not. He didn't do all this emotional stuff well. They said he lacked empathy, which was just a nice way of saying he's an asshole.

"I'll order pizza, and we'll cuddle."

"Blowjob?"

He jerked his gaze to Pure to find the man biting his lips to hide a smile. Little was leaned into Pure's side, and Pure rubbed Little's back.

"Anything you want. I really am sorry."

Pure disconnected the call. "Get the hell out of my house and go get your makeup blowjob."

"Thanks, Pure."

Raul nearly took Little's head off as the man leaned Pure back over his arm, kissing him on the mouth.

"Dude, I know where your mouth has been!"

17

"You ain't gonna tell me you ain't looked at my Poe's ass a time or two."

"He's not exactly my type."

He stood back watching as Little gasped and Pure just smiled sweetly.

"I don't even know who you are."

Little righted Pure and then stormed from the house, the slamming of the door nearly rattling the windows. "Is that all it takes to get rid of him?"

"Usually the promise of a blowjob from Poe and or food. I don't think Little ate everything I heated up."

Pure started to remove the baking sheet from the oven, but he stopped the man. He took the dishtowel and pointed toward the doorway.

"Go take a shower or whatever, I can take care of myself. Just point me in the direction of the important things."

Pure turned to the side and pointed toward the large entryway leading to the living room. "Well, go down that hall, guest bathroom is the first on the right, towels and extra stuff is in the hall closet. Bedroom is across from the bathroom. Gym is in the basement, everything is dusty, though. Did you need something to sleep in?"

"No," he answered and hated that his voice sounded harsh. He was too used to his own company.

"Okay."

"I'm probably just gonna crash. I'll need to check on you every couple of hours, make sure to leave your door unlocked."

Pure acted as if he wanted to complain, but he gave the beautiful man a look that dared him to argue. Then he was left alone in the kitchen to make his plate, and he just stood at the counter eating. Typically, dinner was from any fast-food place he passed on the way back to his extended stay motel. He kept telling himself that he'd get a place—settle in and claim a spot where he didn't feel as if he was constantly on the run.

He finished his last bite of food and turned around in order to wash what he used quickly. He'd always had a habit of leaving no trace of himself behind as if he were no more than a ghost. Permanence was an oddity to him. Even as a child, he hadn't felt as if he belonged anywhere. He'd taken a job that made sure he never had to settle in one place, until this one.

Freelancing for Trenton Security was a lucrative arrangement, but that hadn't factored into the reason he took the full-time job. He knew he couldn't have Pure, yet he also couldn't resist being around him. The sweetness of the man was something he'd never experienced before. Pure held fast to his morals. Never even playfully hinted at having sexual thoughts while everyone around them openly talked about sex.

The last mission they'd been on together to find Gage's niece had opened his eyes to something. There was more to Pure's aversion to sex than just waiting for the right person. They'd shared a room with double beds the two nights they were on the assignment, and each night Pure had cried out in his sleep. He hadn't said a word about it.

He strode through the house making his way to Pure's bedroom. He smiled when he found the door open like he'd ordered and he leaned onto the door frame. Pure's wide chest and curved belly were covered in thick hair. It was the first time he'd seen the man shirtless. He took a moment to study the ink that covered Pure's arms from knuckles to shoulders. They were an abstract scene that changed the more he stared. He made out hints of bodies, shapes that could've represented forests or warzones. There was a single tattoo that ran the length of Pure's ribs. He eased into the room and saw the beautiful script writing. *Strength is being able to love past the pain.* He read the words and felt his brows draw together.

He tensed as Pure shifted in his sleep, and the sheet slipped to expose superhero briefs. He rolled his lips between his teeth to keep from chuckling. The large adorable man was his only weakness. Big and soft, ruthless when he needed to be, and he wanted Pure more than he had anyone else. It was difficult to remember he couldn't have the man.

"Raul, what are you doing?"

Pure rolled to his side and hugged a pillow to his chest. The man rubbed his scruffy cheek against the stark white pillowcase. He looked so innocent and beautiful. He felt so possessive of the bigger man. "Was going to check on you before I jumped in the shower."

"There's sweatpants in the bottom drawer if you want them."

"Thanks." He didn't linger in case Pure figured out he'd been watching him sleep for a few minutes longer than he should have. It had become a frustrating habit. He knew that the rest of the team thought they had a thing for each other. Little took every chance to trap them together. The last time was in the gun locker in the basement of Trenton Headquarters, and Little had decided they needed a sex talk with puppets. He was going to kill that fucker one of these days.

He chuckled to himself as he dug the sweatpants out and hurried to the bathroom to shower, then crash for the night. He'd have to be up every couple of hours to check on Pure. He was looking forward to it. Being able to stay in Pure's space only briefly was a guilty pleasure, and he'd enjoy it until things went back to normal.

DAY WITH THE CREW BABIES

*P*ure opened the door before the knock sounded, and there were babies everywhere. He grabbed the double stroller with Crave and Twitch's twins inside. They were still in the eat, sleep, and poop stage. He didn't care because Lila and Annette were perfect. Once he had them pulled inside, he took Loco, Mary and Bear's toddler, and cuddled him. Mary just shook her head at him. Elisabeth and Ricky were holding hands as they entered. They were both carried by the same surrogate, so they favored each other except for Elisabeth's dark brown skin and Ricky's lighter complexion.

He loved baby days.

"You sure you're up for this? You had a rough day."

He shook his head at Mary. "I'm fine. I don't even have a headache." He looked forward to his day off. Normally he had the whole crew of kids from youngest to the oldest—Juvie was in her twenties, and Princess was almost twenty.

When he was younger, he'd dreamed of finding a man to love and having a big family. That wasn't in the cards anymore, but his nieces and nephews were the highlight of his life.

"I have everything to make cookies and decorate them. I

rented the newest kid's movie. It's all planned out. Have they had breakfast yet?"

"No, they're probably starving. Loco had some apple slices while I made Bear's lunch. Just call if it's too much."

"I promise. Now leave." He shooed Mary, and she shook her head at him.

He didn't want to be rude, but he wanted Mary to go before Raul woke up. It would be all over the Crews if Mary saw Raul coming from the direction of his bedroom. Luckily, she left without further protest, and he leaned down to gently nudge the little girls to the kitchen. He had to get breakfast started. He was a bit tired and sore, but he needed the distraction of the kids, and they were always good. He rolled the stroller and turned it around in front of the patio door. Then he pulled the stools out, got each of the older kids settled with coloring books and crayons, and propped up his tablet for them to watch cartoons.

He gave them each a handful of dry cereal to keep them occupied until he finished the food. He also had another mouth to feed. He placed the bacon on a baking sheet after preheating the oven. He carried on a conversation with the kids as he chopped vegetables for omelets for him and Raul. The kids would get scrambled.

He was just mixing the eggs when he froze at the sight of Raul coming through the kitchen doorway. That was a sight he'd never dreamed he'd see—a sleepy, half-naked man in his home. Raul was nothing but ripped muscle. He'd been around physically perfect men before, but none of them had been in his house or had six-pack abs under smooth light chestnut skin. The pants were low enough to show off the top of Raul's pubes; thick, black, and tight. He tore his gaze from the man and went back to preparing breakfast like he wasn't trying to calm his heart enough to breathe. His face was already flaming, and he wasn't in the mood to embarrass himself.

"We have guests." Raul stopped at the stroller first, stroked chubby cheeks lightly so as not to wake them up.

"Today is my day to babysit. Crew kids are only watched by Crew." He answered as he opened the cabinet above the coffeemaker and grabbed Raul a mug. He filled the mug and turned around to hand it to Raul. The man took his coffee black and strong enough to eat through the mug.

"Thanks."

He held his breath as he waited for Raul to take a sip. It was stupid he knew, but he couldn't deny he had a crush on the other man. His first since high school and it was completely inappropriate. He was sure the big biker had his choice of partners. The Crews weren't shy about sex, and Raul's bisexuality was well known. They'd been on assignments and hitting a bar to relax at the end was a ritual. He'd watched the man flirt with everyone, once or twice seen him leave with men and women. They were always beautiful and slim, and he'd always been a big guy, a bit on the chunky side. He was the opposite of what Raul looked for in a sex partner.

"Coffee is perfect. I know when you make it at work."

He was about to say thank you when Raul turned away and leaned on the counter to smile at the kids. Raul made over their pictures they were drawing. Gushed over their color choice. The man even straightened to move behind each one to give hugs. He'd never seen Raul with the younger kids. Mainly Raul taught the older ones skills that kids really didn't need. Pride, Linus' son, had already learned how to pick locks and the best entry points for a break-in. Well, he couldn't say much, Pride was already a natural with a sniper rifle.

Okay, he admitted that he liked being the cool uncle. He even beat out Little for the distinction, but Raul was maybe a bit ahead of him.

"Uncle Pure," Loco called his name without looking up from the coloring book.

He was an adorable mini-version of Bear. Already tall for his age, he had his tongue between his teeth as if coloring inside the lines took all his concentration.

"Yes, baby?"

"Can I have bear pancakes?"

"Of course, you get bear pancakes, so you want them with bowties?"

"Yes! Blueberries for eyes."

"You got it." He leaned down and placed a quick kiss on Loco's baby soft hair. Spending time with the Crew kids was sometimes bittersweet. It reminded him of what he wanted but wouldn't possess. With Raul there, it was particularly painful. He imagined the scene playing out with a few changes, and he closed his eyes to picture it. Instead of Raul on the other side of the kitchen, Raul would be next to or behind him, strong arms around him.

Before he'd joined Trenton, he'd held onto that little piece of himself that still wanted a normal life. The spiral began when he was barely fifteen. He still remembered the pain and panic, the cop with his disapproving gaze. Minutes of sexual assault had colored the last fifteen years of his life and taken years to work through. He was terrified of what that meant. Kieran Dahl, the local shrink, told him that he needed to be honest when he opened his life to a partner. The right one would understand his limits.

"Ba...Pure, why don't you go lie back down. I can finish breakfast."

Gentle fingers drew down the indent of his spine, and his eyes flew open as he realized he'd lost himself in his thoughts. "No, I'm fine. You won't make Loco's pancakes right." He went back to getting breakfast ready for them.

"You're probably right."

He didn't look at Raul. The years they've worked together intensified his feelings for the other man. But Raul was confident, handsome, in touch with who he was, and Pure was—

Pure. All he had was his job and Crews, all the friends he'd made. It was all rather sad; terror and envy were an odd thing. He'd watched most of his friends partner up, studied the way they cared for their person, and he envied the joy and connection— even the sex.

Strong hands came to rest on his hips as he stood at the stove. Hot breath fanned his ear. "You need—"

"I'm fine. I live for Hellion days. It's all planned out. I can rest when they watch a movie later."

"I'm sticking around just in case."

He barely controlled a groan. He'd expected Raul to leave after breakfast. Raul moved away, and he relaxed as he finished up everything. Once the plates were filled and he got the kids to the table, he pointed to a chair for Raul to sit down. They were all settled in to eat, so he kept himself busy by talking to the kids and refused to look at the other man who sat opposite him at the other end of the table.

The smile on his face felt forced, and he knew it was because he couldn't get used to kids and a man of his own. When they were done, the kids helped him dry dishes, and then they ran outside to play on the equipment he'd built a few years ago.

"You're really good with them."

"Thanks. I always thought I'd have a couple of my own."

"You want kids?"

"Yeah, I want a husband and kids. Mom always told me I'd find the right one someday."

"You mind if I use your shower?"

Raul wasn't subtle about the subject change. "You got clothes?"

"Yeah, in my truck. We'll have to get yours later."

"That's okay. Little will come by. I'm hanging out with Poe, Fielding, Elijah, Brody, well, I'm hanging out with all the partners tonight."

"Do you think you should be out drinking? You need to take it easy."

"I'm a grown-ass man. I can take care of myself. You want to pull that Dominant Daddy bullshit with me...you can take your ass elsewhere."

He started for the backdoor to play with the kids, but Raul grabbed his wrist. The callouses felt good on his skin.

"Nicolas, you don't want to fuck with me, boy. You have a goddamn concussion, and you need to rest. If you want to be stubborn, that's on you, but if you want to fight me, you won't win."

Raul released him and left the room. The man's guttural voice had turned even rougher when he'd spoken. He didn't like when people were mad at him, especially Raul. The man had acted as his spotter and partner for years, so they had to trust each other. And he did, he didn't know why, but out of all his friends, he always trusted Raul to have his back.

He'd apologize later, but first, he had to focus on the kids. They weren't exactly friends. Outside of work, they didn't hang out except with the other Trenton guys. He was too scared to get close to the man. He couldn't allow his feelings to deepen, but he feared he was already too far gone. Maybe he could talk to Gage? He needed someone to give him advice and Gage knew how to keep his mouth shut.

NO FUCKING WAY

*H*e signed the paperwork as two cops took his handcuffed captive back toward the cells. He'd been away from Pure for almost seven days, and he was impatient to get home. While he sent Pure texts and called, he also made sure someone always kept him informed of Pure's whereabouts and that he was safe. Ordering them to take Pure out of the field when he wasn't around wasn't going to make Linus happy.

Pure was the only man to have at your Six. He made his way outside to his truck, then he quickly made his way back to his motel. His mind kept going back to the last morning with Pure. Pure had looked so at home with a baby on his hip or talking to the kids as they colored. He had to keep reminding himself that the sun that was Pure wasn't meant for him.

He didn't know if he could give the man the life he deserved. He'd briefly had a conversation with Gage before he'd left. Domination was natural for him, and he loved a bed partner who understood that he was in control. Yet, Pure required something else from him, and Gage had outlined his doubts without blinking an eye.

. . .

"Is this heart to heart about our resident innocent?"

"I stayed with him yesterday, and some of the Hellions came to spend the day with him."

"You liked being in his kitchen surrounded by babies?"

"I've wanted him for so long. Years, but because of who he is, I can't—"

"You can do whatever you want, man."

"I can't have him, Gage. Owning him would be too much. Possessing the brightest, purest light."

"So poetic."

"Fuck you. What would you do?"

"I already got one boy. I can't handle another. I'm not as young as I used to be. But Pure would make a beautiful addition."

His fists clenched at the thought of someone else possessing Pure. Even joking about it was too much, but he forced himself to relax. He needed Gage's help, and the only thing he could do was be honest. *"I'm not good enough for him."*

"Raul, I thought the same thing when it came to Derrick. Some days it's easier, but others, I'm still fighting my instincts to protect him from me. From what a life with me will be. He has to put up with my self-harm. What's in my head can't be fixed. As much as he wants to, he can't love me whole again. He just has to be there. No relationship is guaranteed for success. Some shit just needs to be worked at, and the people involved just need to love the ugly with the beautiful. If someone can't love and accept the dark parts, then they can't love you a hundred percent.

"If you think you can't do that for Pure, walk away and just stay his friend. What would you rather have?"

As much as he understood Gage was right, the thought of another person touching Pure enraged him, and he couldn't think of walking away. That was a feeling he'd grown used to, and it was something he'd yet to learn how to handle. Being possessive wasn't natural for him. Fucking had always been just that—fucking. But with Pure, he knew it would be a promise. Pure had waited for the right one, and he was so far from Mr. Right.

He was ready to go home. He pulled into the motel and cast a glance to the truck stop across the parking lot. He could use a beer and food before he headed home. Once his stomach was full, and he grabbed some coffee, he'd pack up his truck and head out. The room went mainly unused, but he'd leave a nice tip for the housekeeper that came the next morning. He'd hung in enough motels to know the housekeepers made shit for nasty work.

His life was one motel to another. He needed to think about making his life in Powers more permanent. He'd signed on with Linus full-time but still did some freelance stuff when he needed. The moment he felt trapped, he left without thought of who he hurt. He hadn't seen his parents in years because they didn't understand him and didn't love all of him. In his teens, he'd acted out to put his masculinity and straightness above reproach, fucked women just to prove he wasn't gay.

He'd hated himself for years, and it wasn't until he'd started working with the Trenton Crew that he'd accepted his bisexuality. When they were out on jobs, he'd taken men and women back to his room. But he'd never felt satisfied. His guilt had grown the longer he'd spent around Pure. Being with Pure had quickly turned into an impossibility when he'd learned Pure was innocent and waiting around for *the one*. He wasn't that man. Attempting to fuck Pure out of his system with any willing body hadn't worked.

His thoughts suddenly made his appetite disappear, and he decided to pack up his things. All he wanted to do was go home and be around Pure. There was something about Pure that made everything in him settle, but he didn't want to trust the feeling.

Pessimism had kept him from pursuing Pure. He'd resigned himself to just soaking up Pure's presence and hoped it would be enough. He entered his musty motel room and grabbed his toiletry bag from the bathroom and shoved it into his still packed duffle bag. He'd just pick up some fast-food on the road.

He left the card key on the dresser and left. Once he was on the road, he turned the radio on. Music blasting for the long ride home.

FOUR CAR ACCIDENTS AND ONE QUICK POWER NAP, HE ARRIVED back at his motel just outside Powers. He wanted to drop off his bag and then get some actual sleep before he had to be back at the office in the morning. He kicked off his boots as he slammed the door behind him. His bag was carelessly tossed to land beside the round dining table. Even the lumpy bed with the ugly bedspread looked amazing at this point.

He stretched out and pushed a long sigh between his compressed lips. As exhausted as he was, his brain went into hyperdrive. Life before Powers and Pure was dangerous but easy —he did his job, and he moved on to the next motel. Permanence and happily ever afters had never come into play. He'd started to question the decisions he'd made in his existence.

Pure was the person he felt he could make room in his life for, but it also terrified him. Gage's words kept playing through his head. Was he willing to let Pure go? Someone would come in and take Pure from him. Each time he thought about the possibility, the more enraged he became. But he was fearful that he couldn't be the man Pure needed. His dominance would terrify the other man. He'd observed Pure for too long not to have picked up on the subtleties of his triggers.

The operation they'd gone on with Gage had shown him the full extent of Pure's inhibitions. Something as minor as a sexual spanking made him spiral. He hadn't met a person he'd have to restrain his urges with before. Being a Daddy or a Dominant was just part of him, and it was as natural as breathing for him. As much as he wanted to be what Pure needed, he just didn't know if he could hide an entire aspect of him—not even for Pure. He seemed destined for failure. Would it be fair to either of them to pretend?

If Pure was his, he'd show him that there wasn't shame in what they were to each other. He'd seen the potential in Pure. The hidden submissive; but in Pure's mind, allowing himself to be controlled equaled demeaning the man he thought he was.

He closed his eyes as he imagined Pure curled up to his side. Every night he went to sleep, his tired brain would conjure his dream boy. The big, soft man cuddled against him as they fell asleep. He still couldn't get past how hard it was becoming to resist.

The real world slid away, and his secret happy place took over. In his mind, he held Pure closer. Pressed his lips to Pure's forehead and traced the curve of the bigger man's smile with the pad of his thumb. He relaxed every muscle starting with his neck and worked slowly down to his toes as he let himself slip into the dream world where he was allowed to own his boy.

HE JERKED AS A HEAVY HAND BANGED ON THE DOOR, AND HE awakened to see that the morning light barely illuminated the space around the curtains. He rolled from the bed, seeing it was just after sunrise, and he'd slept for several hours. He threw open the door.

"What the fuck do y'all want?" he demanded as he saw two uniformed deputies standing there with their hands on their weapons. It was two Powers County Officers that he hadn't seen before, but him and the Trenton guys didn't mix with anyone but Linus' husband, Wren, and Sheriff Pelter.

"Raul Martinez?"

"Yeah, like I said, what y'all want?"

"You're under arrest, please step outside."

He opened his mouth to demand to know what the hell was going on, and then he had two weapons in his face. The bigger deputy had him spun and slammed against the wall beside the door.

"What am I under arrest for?" He grimaced as the zip cuffs cut into his wrists.

"Homicide."

Everything in him froze when one of them answered him. From experience, he didn't have a comeback, and he knew to keep his mouth closed until he got representation. He'd stay quiet until he was in the same room with Pelter. What happened in the last twenty-four hours since he'd driven out of Texas? He had more enemies than he could count. The threats he'd received even outnumbered them. After a while, he found the promises of death were just part of the job.

He allowed them to drag him to the marked cruiser. Law enforcement didn't play when it came to homicide suspects. He had to believe Peaches and the guys would get him out of this. Placing his trust in them was all he had, and the sooner he arrived at the Sheriff's department, the sooner they could straighten everything out. Although, his first thought was getting someone to Pure before the news hit him by surprise.

THEY COULDN'T WAIT AND SEE

*A*n hour ago, when he'd stood on the firing line to do some thinking, he hadn't thought he'd get up the courage to talk to Gage. The other man had said if he ever wanted to talk, but it had seemed easier in his head when he'd planned out what he wanted to say.

"You going to stand in my doorway all day or tell me why you're staring at me?"

"You said if I ever needed to talk..."

"Come in and close the door. They'll think Derrick came to tell Daddy hi and will leave us alone."

He closed the door and turned to lean back on the smooth surface, the wood cool through his t-shirt. He'd never said the words out loud before. Even when he'd talked to his mom, he'd refused to name it. *Rape.* He still didn't know if he was prepared to whisper the one word that had caused him years of shame, but he was curious about something. Too many years he'd trapped himself in a mental prison. How was he supposed to step outside his comfort zone when the natural act of sex made him feel dirty?

"Why are you a Daddy?"

Gage steepled his fingers, and the longer Gage stared at him, the more nervous he got. "Because it allows me to show a part of me that I've always hidden away. I can love on my boy and care for him, and he gifts me with unquestionable trust to know what's best for him."

"What would my Daddy be like?"

He knew it was different for everyone. Pelter was the sweet and compassionate one with his boys. He made sure Sin and Saint were always happy and content. Bull tended to be heavy-handed with Gregory, but that was only because Bull's husband liked it. Livingston took complete control of Fielding, Liv made all decisions in their marriage, but that's what Fielding needed.

He was intrigued by giving up that control. His life was mostly lived through the scope of his sniper rifle. Everything within that small frame he could count on. His peace was measured in velocity, airspeed, and feet per second—everything else was an unknown variable that he couldn't account for—that was the part of his life that terrified him.

"Well, it depends on what kinda Daddy that you're drawn to. But in the end, it's up to the boy on what Daddy he needs. Derrick needs me to be loving but forceful, to make sure he's always safe and loved. He needs to be grounded, and when he disobeys, he needs me to take him in hand and instruct him."

"What kinda Daddy would I need?" The question fell unsteadily from his trembling lips. It was the question he had feared but always seemed compelled to ask.

"Caring and compassionate, one to love the shadows from your eyes. If anyone took the time to look, they'd understand you were hurt before you came to them. And while you're bruised a bit, a little TLC can make you beautiful."

He bit his lip shyly at being called beautiful. Men weren't supposed to be that, but all the Daddies called their boys that.

"Pure, if you name it, it no longer has power over you."

He didn't know if he believed Gage. His brain wanted to

ignore it, pretend it never existed, and go on with his life as is. Did he want to trust Raul that much—could he? But what if Gage was right, just saying it could help him move forward.

"I allowed myself to be—"

"Boy, you're not mine, but I will put you over my knee if you finish that."

He steadied his voice. Brought his thoughts down to the squeeze of the trigger and breathed the truth aloud for the first time in years. He closed his eyes and just said it. "I was raped."

When he opened them to look at Gage, he didn't see judgment or pity.

"And that had nothing to do with you. The fucker wanted control and power...to break you down. It's your choice in life whether to allow a single man to destroy you. Love allows us to transcend all the darkness that we pull around us to protect ourselves from the unknown. Love is your unknown, Pure. You were unable to allow yourself to be seen as a being that requires intimacy."

"What if it hurts?"

"Pure, listen to me very carefully. Your Daddy will want nothing more than your pleasure. And if he doesn't, then he's not the one for you. You will discuss your limits. You will be honest about what is acceptable for your body and comfort. If he doesn't want to adhere to those and doesn't give you a safe word, then walk away. The boy has all the power. With a single word, a boy can make his Daddy heel. And if he doesn't, I'll teach him very clearly what safe, sane, and consensual means."

"What if I can't just let go?"

"Pure, any man, Daddy Dom or not, will respect your limits. I will say it again. The sub will always have the power. Just because a man claims to own you doesn't mean you have to follow blindly."

"But I've said horrible things and treated y'all differently for what you do, I feel like a hypocrite."

"We're all about forgiveness. Mistakes are made. It's how we grow from them. I treated my boy horribly, but he saw past all the barriers I threw up. Raul—"

"What's this have to do with him?"

Gage's deep chuckle filled the office. "Boy, you can't hide that you were asking because of your partner. We've all seen it over the years. You have to be open and honest with him. While I've assumed your inhibitions were more than just saving your first time for the right man, I'm not sure that anyone else noticed or delved any deeper than that."

He was about to open his mouth and deny it until the banging on the office door had him jumping.

"Conference room now." Livingston's voice boomed easily through the heavy wooden door.

Then they were in movement and jogging from the office and down the hall to the main conference room. Gage and he were the last ones to enter. Linus' expression cut off any line of questioning. The look on Peaches' face especially said that something bad had happened. His stomach churned as he realized the only member not there was Raul, but he wasn't due back from Texas until the following day.

"Before everyone loses their shit, I'm taking care of it, but we have to discuss what is going on. You're a tight crew. You'll want to run in and save the day. All that will do is make the situation worse." Peaches spoke as Linus stepped to the side to allow her center stage.

He wrung his hands as he waited for the news.

"Raul has been charged with first-degree murder and was arrested three hours ago at his motel room."

He opened his mouth to demand more information, but she held up her hand, cutting him off. Her look freezing him in place. That silent order was only for him.

"All the evidence at this point in the investigation is circumstantial but strong enough for them to issue a warrant. We have twenty-four hours before Texas Marshals arrive to extradite him back for his arraignment. What we know is that the victim was a twenty-five-year-old bartender who Raul was seen speaking to and possibly flirting with."

He tried not to be hurt, Raul wasn't his, but it wouldn't be the first bartender Raul had taken home after an assignment.

"His body was found in Raul's room by the motel manager. It appears the victim was beaten to death. Another guest called in a noise complaint, and when the manager arrived, a male fitting Raul's build was seen exiting the room. I've already talked to a friend in Texas who's going to meet us there."

"What the fuck do you mean, meet us there? No fucking way am I letting him—"

"You're officially off this assignment, Pure." The order was clear in Linus' tone.

When he started to argue, Gage grabbed his bicep and ordered him to stand down. He didn't want to remain calm. They couldn't let Raul leave the state.

"We just have to wait and see. You're too close to this one, Pure. We want you out of this. If you even try to put your nose into this, I will fire you."

He opened his mouth to tell Linus to fuck off, but Gage's grip became painful. If they threw him out, he'd be out of the loop completely. He needed details, and his time was limited. Twenty-four hours wasn't long enough to come up with a plan.

"Right now, I'm using a stall tactic. I can fight the extradition. I'll lose, but it'll earn us some extra time. We're headed to the Sheriff's station in order to check on him and start the process of his defense. I can't have y'all showing y'all's asses, I need to know what they have."

Peaches talked out what they were going to do and filled them in on the attorney who would handle things outside her jurisdiction. She was ready to travel at any time, but until then, she'd fight to keep Raul in Georgia. He didn't give a fuck if they needed to wait and see, that was utter bullshit, and he wasn't going to sit still. He'd sit in on the meeting, but as soon as that happened, he was on his own. He wasn't going to let his partner and spotter be taken down. First, he needed to figure out why, and be prepared to take the kill shot.

RAUL'S FATE AWAITED

*H*e paced the small enclosure of his cell and tried to ignore Pelter watching him. A transport was coming the next day to take him back to Texas. He still couldn't get over them arresting him at his motel. When the Crew arrived with Peaches, Pure's gaze had met his through the aged-stained glass, and when he'd stepped out of the interrogation room, everything came down to just Pure. He swore Pure was about to guard him when the man's hand went for his sidearm. Gage had whispered in Pure's ear, and the man relaxed, but that intense focus never left him.

"I didn't do this, Cam."

"Not at any point did I believe you did, but the evidence is more than circumstantial."

"I can account for every step I made while I was there. Except for the night I left to head home. No one saw me for the last five hours of travel time."

When he'd left, his room was almost like he hadn't been there at all. Whoever did this would've had to wait for him to leave. What if he had stayed the night? Would his body have been found along with the victim? When the cops had questioned him, he'd recognized the kid in the photos. Even covered in blood, he recognized the beautiful face of the bartender from the restaurant he'd eaten at a few times.

He'd flirted, and the kid had even given him a napkin with his number on it. The flirting had been innocent enough, but not once had he thought about asking the young man back to his room. He'd stopped hooking up a year ago, when he'd only signed on as freelance with Trenton, it had been easier to ignore his attraction.

"Someone saw me talking with the kid, but I don't know why anyone would want to jack me up with fake charges. I was on the road to come home."

"Did you talk to anyone? Your cell records would give locations."

"No, it was late, and I drove straight through, took a break for a power nap when I wasn't in traffic due to accidents and stops for coffee. I wanted to get back."

"Anyone stand out?"

"No, I mean, I get threats all the time. I take down people on the run. The list is long."

"Peaches will take care of it."

"She's not licensed to practice in Texas."

"That hasn't stopped her before, and she has a lot of friends, and she told you she already arranged for an attorney."

She had and an entire list of other things. The last twelve hours was a haze of panic and worry. It was like Raul's world had shrunk down to a single focus, but there was something—someone—more important.

"Is Pure okay?"

"He left town."

"Where the fuck did he go? Linus better not have sent him on a job without me." He wrapped his hands around the bars and squeezed until his knuckles turned white. Pure never went out on his own. It was the one thing he'd demanded when he'd signed on full-time. No one else would act as the man's partner, which was kind of shitty on his part because he'd gone on plenty of assignments without Pure. Those were mainly made when he needed a break from controlling himself around the younger man.

"Calm the fuck down. He's not handling the plans well, and he went home to his mom's. Pure wasn't agreeing with the setup to let you be taken back to Texas. He thought they should fight harder to keep you here until more evidence came in."

"More evidence? They found a murdered young man in my motel room with witnesses that said me and the vic were getting cozy. They might as well strap me in for lethal injection now."

"Knock it off. Shit, you gotta keep your head on straight. You lose it, and Pure will too. You two are linked or something."

They'd always worked as a seamless unit. They could go carry out a complete operation without uttering a single word. He had to keep fighting because his beautiful partner needed him. Being on the inside would leave Pure vulnerable.

"He just left?"

"Let's just say it wasn't easy. I think they threatened to fire him, so they called Jenn to order him home."

In the years they'd been partnered up, Pure had never introduced him to his mother. It wasn't until he'd gone to Pure's house that he'd learned what the woman looked like. He wondered if there was a reason for that. He could understand keeping a separation between work and personal, but in the Crews, lines were crossed all the time.

"Do you think he thinks I did it?"

"No one thinks you did it, man, especially not Pure. He doesn't let anyone at his back, and I've seen you two work together. The trust is right there in your face. I think he feels powerless because he's been ordered not to help. They didn't even want him in on meetings. At this point, that boy is ready to take everyone out. Him and Liv tangled, and I think shots were almost fired. At that point, they called his mama."

He didn't like that he was making Pure lose his calm. He'd found the act of Pure lining up a shot the sexiest thing in the world. The focus and serenity—that single soft exhale as Pure gently squeezed the trigger. It was almost like meditation for Pure. In the moment Pure fired, he was at his most confident— his place of peace. The shy man he wanted to dominate turned into a brutally constrained killing machine. The dichotomy of Pure's two halves were the first things that drew him.

He hugged the bars and leaned his forehead on two of them. He should be worried about spending the rest of his life in prison —maybe dying for a crime he didn't commit, but his thoughts were as they always were—focused on Pure. He couldn't leave his boy alone. He couldn't allow someone else to protect him, but he didn't have a say in what happened until he stood before a judge, and his bail was decided.

His background and job made him a flight risk, not to mention he was charged with a viciously violent crime. Beating someone to death wasn't a few shots center mast or a slit throat, a physical altercation meant a crime of passion. An intense hatred or just an unknown person who took pleasure in the pain they inflicted.

Keeping Pure away from this was best, he agreed with Linus and Peaches' logic, but that put Pure out in the cold with no one to watch his back. That was his job. He was always supposed to keep his boy safe and unharmed, but being locked up put Pure in danger.

He felt regret for not keeping his promise to always protect Pure. He'd left the road behind to exist in Pure's presence, not even to possess him. He craved being there in his space.

"He'll be fine, man. You'll be back home before you know it."

"I'm not so sure. Someone really did a number, and I have no fucking clue why. Yeah, I've earned some enemies...but why the fuck would they go to all this trouble?"

"Maybe it's not even that. Could be someone wanted to take you out and an innocent got in the way. It wasn't a secret where you were staying, someone could've been waiting for you and when he knocked, attacked before—"

"I'm at least fifty pounds heavier than that boy. There's no mistaking a twinky white boy for the big, mean-ass brown man. They knew what they were doing, I don't know why, and that's what's bugging me the most. I can get someone wanting to take me out. It's part of the gig. That kid didn't do shit but show me a little too much attention in the bar."

"Then fight to avenge him. I checked, and no one's claimed his body yet."

"Tell Peaches to take care of that. Linus has access to my accounts. Have him pull the money. Make sure it's done up all nice for him."

"Will do."

The kid deserved someone to mourn him. Stand by his grave and acknowledge that he existed. He had seen too many people die alone, unloved and forgotten, a numbered marker in a shitty corner of a graveyard. That wouldn't happen on his watch. Someone had used an innocent as a pawn in the plot to take him out. When he was exonerated, he'd make it his mission that the people to blame paid for it. If they wanted to add a body count to his back, then he'd make sure the fucker who beat an innocent kid to death was the first one to go down.

THE GREAT ESCAPE

*P*ure braced the barrel of his sniper rifle on the safety frame of his tree stand. Two days ago, he'd prepared and had kept all the details to himself. Raul wouldn't make it through one night in jail. He'd already heard the rumors. Whoever was after Raul posted a hell of a bounty on his head. The vehicle he'd borrowed was parked two miles away, and they'd have to double-time it to make it before reinforcements converged on the location of the accident. Although, that wouldn't happen until they were on their way to freedom.

He placed signal blockers that would cut all radio and cell communication. Working for Trenton Security had led him up to this moment and had taught him the skills he needed. Raul was his partner—spotter—the man who he'd always trusted at his back. He wasn't going to let some unknown force take Raul down. He checked the display on his forearm that told him he had ten minutes until the prisoner transport broke the point of no return.

Everything he'd purchase for this operation was fresh out of the packaging or provided from shady contacts. All bought with cash and in another town. He hadn't left anything to chance. His mom was ready to cover his whereabouts at the time of the escape. She was the only one who knew what he was doing. His involvement wouldn't stay a secret to his former team for long, but she'd called in an emergency three days ago telling him he needed to come home.

He breathed evenly, found his center—the place he was calmest. Peering through his scope, he spotted the van. Raul was the only prisoner inside. He wouldn't have gone through with his plan any other way. They'd scheduled Raul's pick up to transport him to Texas. While being a part of Trenton had its perks, it also came with a lot of distrust from law enforcement agencies.

He'd seen Raul's face when they'd showed up at the department after the meeting. The uncertainty was clear, and there was no way he could let the other man go down on bogus charges.

He mentally counted down, gently tapped the trigger as he took a deep breath through his nose. On his exhale, he squeezed the trigger and the tire exploded. The van lurched, the driver overcorrected, he aimed again, and as he took out a second tire, the van flipped.

He watched the chaos he'd caused below through his scope as one of the men inside kicked out the windshield. The man staggered as he attempted to try and assess the scene. Pure slung his rifle strap over his shoulder, stood and grabbed the rope as he rappelled to the ground. He took enough time to place his rifle next to his dirt bike. He removed his forty-five caliber from his thigh holster and made his way through the woods then into the clearing. He compressed the trigger to catch the man's attention —his shot connected between his feet.

He shook his head as the man readied himself to fire.

"Drop your weapon and on your knees."

He repeated the order until the officer held his arms to the side, dropped his service weapon, and fell to his knees to the asphalt. He ignored the cursing and orders to stand down as he removed the handcuff keys from the man's pocket and tossed them several feet away. After he was confident that the man was secured to the grille guards, the officer told him he wouldn't get away with whatever he planned. Pure was confident that he'd do just fine until they could figure out who framed Raul.

He didn't want to speak too much in case someone could recognize his voice later. He checked the pulse of the other officer, found the beat strong, so it meant the man was just unconscious. Running to the rear of the tipped vehicle, he unlocked the back with keys he'd taken after checking if the guy was alive or not.

Cursing, he found Raul foolishly trying to break his shackles from the floor. Raul spun toward him, ready to fight and he tossed Raul the keys. Thankfully, Raul didn't question and just started unlocking himself. Pure removed his second weapon and flipped it. He saw the suspicion, but as Raul took it, he backed away. He took off back to the tree line and trusted Raul to follow him. He'd altered the barrels of the weapons, left his rifle behind with the tree stand and hopped on the dirt bike.

"Pure, what the fuck were you thinking?"

"Just get on, we have maybe a fifteen-minute window. You can bitch at me later."

That's all it took, and Raul hopped on behind him, then they were off in the direction of the stashed vehicle. Their combined weights made it awkward to steer the bike, but they made it. He could practically feel the anger rolling off Raul, but they'd have to deal with it when he got them someplace safe.

He slowed, rolled the bike to a stop, and cut the engine off. As fast as he could manage, he thrust a bag with a change of clothes in Raul's direction and a pair of boots.

"These are mine."

"I had Peaches go to your motel room and grab your stuff after we left the Sheriff's department, well, what the cops left. Everything is at my house in the spare room, and your truck is in my garage. A state forensics team came and tested everything, since there seemed to be nothing to connect it to the crime, it was released. They did seize your GPS, though."

"You're going to explain what the hell just went down."

"Sources say there's a hundred-k bounty on your head. Where is it best to take you out?"

"Jail. I didn't kill him."

"I didn't think you did." He stripped out of his tactical gear and stowed it in the trunk. "Get in the backseat and tuck down on the floorboard. We have thirty minutes on the countdown for signals to be restored, that is unless someone sees the accident. I didn't go through all this trouble to get caught."

"You shouldn't have done this. I should put you over my knee."

"Not in this lifetime." He grumbled and got in the driver's seat as he watched Raul in the rearview as the man cursed, but eventually did as he said. Before the door had slammed, he was taking off down the dirt road.

"Where are we going?"

"You'll see."

"What do you know?"

He corrected as the tail end fishtailed on the loose gravel. "First thing I checked was who contracted the fugitive retrieval. The guy's a bit shady, but he came up clean. I thought he might be prone to taking bribes, but I couldn't find anything. We have a ton of files to go through when we get to the safe house. Every fugitive you've taken down and a lot of them made some threats. Most of them are capable or have followed through in the past."

"You're leaving clues."

"Nope. All the equipment was new. I altered all the barrels just in case to change the barrel characteristics. Nothing comes back to me directly. Also, my mom is ready to swear I was with her the last three days."

"Your mom is lying for you?"

"It's not really a lie. I have been at her place for three days. She'll just say I was there all day today."

"Is the team waiting?"

"We're on our own. The less people who knew, the better."

"You did this without them?"

"Yes, they weren't taking the threats seriously. They were going to let my spotter go to jail, and that wasn't happening. You might be able to fight off a few until we could get you out, but with the price on your head...everyone would be gunning for you."

"You should've let me go to jail."

"No, now shut up so I can focus. We have to avoid all major roads until we get where we're going."

He was fine when the man shut up, and he took the pre-planned route. They'd only have to hit the highway when they got closer to the safe house. He had it all planned out to a point. His mom and him had manufactured a believable cover for him being home. Today she was setting up one of her rental properties with electric and water. He'd be working on it to get it ready for the next tenants.

Hadn't the team said it was best for him to take a backseat while they worked on finding whoever wanted Raul dead? They were just going to work it while Raul was trapped inside with hundreds of enemies that wanted to kill him. They considered him a flight risk, and the nature of the murder would keep him confined until trial. That could be months. Raul had put his life on the line for him too many times to let him get shanked in the back for a payday.

He turned on the scanner to check for trouble, and it seemed his luck was holding out or they ordered radio silence to cover their actions. Raul was involved with law enforcement.

He pulled onto one of the main roads and turned off the final turn they'd be on for another thirty minutes before they hit the highway and the rest of the way into the city. He hoped they'd think Raul and his accomplice would head south, but he couldn't make any promises. Life would go back to normal as soon as they found out who was at fault. He'd worry about his future later.

THE BOY NEEDED HIS ASS SPANKED

*H*e was seething from where he was squeezed into the floorboard, and he'd stopped talking to Pure thirty minutes ago. What the hell had the boy been thinking of conducting an operation like this on his own? Not that he wasn't thankful that he wasn't going to have to fight off a couple hundred motherfuckers with a hard-on for a bounty. Still, anything could've gone wrong. He didn't care how good Pure was because all it would've taken was one tiny mistake.

A grunt was forced out of him as the car hit a bump as they turned onto an incline and then it was all dark. The sound of a garage door lowering signaled they'd arrived wherever Pure had taken him.

"Come on. We're safe, but we're moving on tomorrow to a better place. I have to pack in supplies tonight."

Pure's voice was strangely calm as if he hadn't just taken out a prison transport. He wiggled out of the tiny space and onto the backseat, then out the door Pure opened for him. The scent of musty air mixed with faint scents of gas and oil filled his nose. As he slammed the door, he caught Pure opening a door that let bright light into the dark garage.

"Mom, you home?"

"Hey, honey, how was work?"

What the fuck? He ascended the few steps that led into a cheery kitchen with flowery curtains and chocolate wafted on the breeze created by a ceiling fan.

"Seems successful. You stink, go take a shower. Dinner is in thirty."

"I love you too, Ma. House ready for us?"

"I dropped off groceries, and the renovation supplies will be delivered tomorrow or the next day."

"Mom, this is—"

"Go."

"Yes, ma'am."

He didn't know why he smiled at the tiny woman ordering a beast like Pure around, but it was cute how he dragged his feet out of the room. He could almost picture Pure as a little boy being chastised by his mom, and it was adorable, but to be honest, he thought that about Pure a lot. It was one of the reasons his Daddy side found Pure irresistible.

"Hi, I'm Jenn, and you're Raul. I've heard a lot about you."

"Hope some of it was good."

"My son trusts you, so that's all that's important. I wasn't happy about his plan."

"Then why didn't you talk him out of it?"

"Talk him out it?" She scoffed. "I helped him plan it. I made chicken and dumplings for dinner. You can clean up in the downstairs bathroom. I bought and washed you some clothes, along with some shampoo and stuff. Nicolas told me what brands you preferred. Everything is in a duffel in the guest room off the living room."

He didn't know what to say. She looked like the perfect suburban stay-at-home mom with her bun and flowery apron, but she just admitted to planning a felony.

He stepped into the living room, and he froze as a wall of

pictures caught his attention. He approached, and for some reason, he felt his mouth tug into a wide smile. There was a line of pictures that was Pure's mom decked out for Pride, some included Pure, and some didn't.

"Even when he was gone, I never missed Pride."

"My parents wouldn't step foot near Pride." His parents hadn't taken the news of his bisexuality well, and while they still talked, any mention of his personal life was ignored. The few times he'd visited, he'd thought about inviting Pure or at the very least tell them he'd met someone who he believed could've turned out to be his one. Each time he'd decided against it, he couldn't subject Pure to the censure even if it was passive-aggressive. Their conditional love made him demanding of finding someone who would accept every part of him.

"He came out when he was just a wee thing."

"I can't picture Pure as being a wee thing."

"I think at eight, he was already taller than I was."

The love she had for Pure was right there on her face—in the way she stroked his image behind glass. Too much could go wrong, and he'd rather waste away in prison knowing Pure was living his life. Happy and healthy—free.

"He shouldn't have come after me."

"I didn't agree with his decision, but he explained it to me, and I had to support his reasoning."

"You're weird."

"I'm pretty normal compared to Peaches and Lily."

"You've all been in the same room?" He was horrified by the thought. It was bad enough that the Matriarchs of the Crews thought the law was all gray area.

"Plenty of times, but not so much in the last few years. I work the night shift in the ER."

"Stressful job." No wonder she was cool under pressure. Emergency Room nurses were a special breed. From just meeting her, he was sure she could take care of herself.

"Can be, but I love it. They wanted to move me to another department, and I refused."

He needed to address the elephant in the room. "Why are you helping me?" She had no connection to him at all, and anyone else would've told their son he'd lost his mind. That wasn't what she did. She went through the whole process of helping her son plan a felony that would have him going to jail.

"Because my son has never been close to anyone. He trusts you, and that's rare. Go get yourself cleaned up."

"I'm going to turn myself in before the heat comes down on him."

"You'll do what you need to protect him. From all the stories I've heard, you're the only man he'd ever want at his Six, and that's a big thing for Pure. Dinner is on the table in twenty."

He nodded and went to find his room. Once inside, he closed and locked the door behind him. He rested his back against it as everything suddenly played out in his head, but not the version where they ended up there. It was the one where Pure took a bullet or was arrested. He needed to figure out how to turn himself in without implicating Pure. He jumped as a soft knock vibrated the door. He straightened and turned to open it.

On the other side, Pure stood there in a towel around his hips and nothing else. Pure was nibbling on his bottom lip the way he did when he was nervous about something. The bigger man had very few tells, but that was his biggest one.

He stepped back as Pure advanced and started to speak, and then the softest lips he ever felt pressed to his. He didn't even think, just hugged Pure's waist and spread his hands over the damp skin of his lower back. The man whimpered and fisted his big hands in his t-shirt. Resistance was a thing of the past, and he used his leaner body to push Pure against the door. It was like every sweet dream he'd ever had as he teased the seam of Pure's mouth with his tongue. Pure's thick, hard cock ground against his abdomen.

He fisted his hands in Pure's soft wet hair and took control. There was the slightest tensing of Pure's bigger frame, so he eased the kiss.

"I'm okay, baby."

"I was scared." Pure rested his forehead to Raul's, as he traced the plump bottom lip.

Disappointment infused him. He'd wanted a kiss incited by need and not one of relief. The hard-on was caused by an untried body being stimulated. He needed to put distance between them before they made a mistake. His life would be harder now. He knew the weight of Pure's body, the softness of his chest hair and the way the cute curve of his belly gave. What would torture him the most was the trembling of lush lips and a sexy whimper.

It took everything in him to step away, but he couldn't go far. Pure looked vulnerable where he was rested back against the bedroom door. His gaze taking in everything but him, Pure's embarrassment was clear.

"Thank you for what you did."

"You're not mad?" Pure's voice went all soft and sweet.

"I am, but you have to understand, if it's between me going to jail and you going, I'm sacrificing myself. You have to let me do that."

"I don't agree."

The boy I knew him to be disappeared in those three short words. His partner was back, and his thick arms were crossed over his broad chest.

"I don't care what you agree to. You're earning spankings the longer you fight me."

He forced himself not to snort at the bratty eye roll, and then Pure was opening the door. The big man turned to glance over his shoulder.

"Tomorrow morning, we head to one of my mom's rental properties. I agreed to do some of the renovations to get it ready to lease. There's a hidden room in the basement. It's a safe place for you to hide if they come looking for you through me. I didn't plan this to have you go to jail and die on me. You might think you'll win, but Gage said the boy is always in charge."

Before he had a chance to respond, the door slammed, and he was alone in his borrowed room. He reached for his phone to call Gage and find out what the hell he'd told Pure, then realized he didn't have it and also that he couldn't contact the team. Was Pure kissing him more than being caught up in the moment? Had his boy, that he'd secretly wanted, made the first move?

Life was way too complicated, and he couldn't think with his dick. He had to keep them both alive and free. Then he'd figure out what the hell happened in the days he spent locked up. Apparently, Pure was talking to Gage about things that weren't the older man's business. Gage had his own boy and needed to leave Pure alone. Confusion changed swiftly to anger. Pure was his, and if he wanted a Daddy, he was the only one Pure was going to get.

HE'D MADE THE FIRST MOVE

*A*fter he'd left Raul's room, nausea had threatened to take him down. He'd stood in the shower, and the adrenaline had quickly ebbed away. All the shit that could've gone wrong had played out, and he'd impulsively went to find Raul. When the other man had opened the door, all he could think about was finding out what Raul's lips felt like. He wasn't one to take the lead, but he was tired of the fear—of pretending he was okay with his loneliness.

He wanted to experience the connections his friends had with their people. Just a kiss had made his body react embarrassingly fast. That's why he was hiding in his workroom in the basement. He'd just finished reloading his 50 calibers for his sniper rifle. The process of reloading his own ammo always calmed him, but now that he was done, he couldn't hide anymore. He was waiting for his mom to get up for her night shift before they left for the safehouse.

A knock sounded behind him. "Come in."

He didn't turn around as the door creaked open and he pretended to clean the already spotless bench, then put away his supplies.

"You're hiding."

"Not really, I just needed to—"

"You have enough ammo stockpiled for the zombie apocalypse."

"You can never be too prepared."

A shiver ran up his spine as Raul chuckled in that sexy rasp of his, and he tried to suppress it. He could clock the man's every movement around his small room. He turned his head to find Raul checking out the pictures from his competitions. His mom had worked too many years in the ER to ever be completely comfortable with his chosen profession, but she was proud of what he'd accomplished.

"When do we head out?"

"Just after dark. The house is only about five minutes away in a quiet suburb. Luckily, the tenants moved out, and Mom just hadn't gotten around to getting it ready."

He stood up from his stool and started packing his weapons and ammo he wanted to take with him. Fingertips stroked down his back, and he froze seconds before Raul pressed to his back.

"What was this Gage said about the boy is always in charge?"

Strong hands took hold of his hips, and he felt as if his throat was closing. The panic built in the center of his chest and he spun, upset with himself. Too many times to remember Raul had gone into buildings behind him and not an ounce of fear had taken over, but in this, it was different—a new dynamic.

"He said a Daddy would respect my limits, but I had to be honest." His voice was barely above a whisper. "I can't promise I won't get scared or nervous. But I...I trust you." He fought Raul's attempt to tip his head back.

"Boy, look at me."

He felt the compulsion to argue, to reestablish his control, but Gage said he needed to be open. He didn't know if he could. Gage was the first person he'd told, the doctors, nurses, and cops had told his mother. Voicing it made it too real. It was always a memory for his nightmares.

"There's those beautiful blue eyes."

He'd never heard that tone from Raul before, or seen that particular tilt to the corner of his mouth. Thinking about his lips brought back their first kiss. He'd always been a big man. Tall and broad, and he knew what people saw when they looked at him. But inside, he always wanted to find that one man for his happily ever after. His brain had claimed Raul as the one, and he still didn't know how he felt about that.

"Baby, I can't put your fears at ease if I don't know what they are. Daddies aren't mind-readers, we don't automatically know what our boys need." Raul's voice deepened.

Pure held his breath as Raul closed the distance between their mouths. The kiss was light and chaste. It was a soothing act, not a seductive one. Raul's hands came up to cup his bearded jaw. This wasn't the time or place for them to accept a mutual need, but he'd come too close to losing Raul.

"I've thought about kissing you way too long." Raul slanted his mouth across his, and he whimpered as the slightly shorter man nipped at his lower lip.

His hands shook as he brought them to Raul's waist where he fisted them in the man's t-shirt. His breathing was too ragged, and his heart kicked into high gear as he was manhandled until he was seated on the bench table. He caught Raul's wrists as the man released his face and tried to slip beneath his t-shirt.

"It's okay, only as fast as you want."

The soft, caring tone was his undoing. He rubbed the soft cotton of Raul's shirt between his fingers.

"We use our words, boy, and you look at me when you talk to me."

He lifted his chin from where he rested it on his chest and forced himself to meet Raul's gaze.

"We have a lot to talk about. Too much planning to do, but

right now, we're going to forget what's happening outside this room and focus on this right here."

"When we went after Alex's daughter, Gage said his door was always open if I wanted to talk about what was bothering me."

"We're partners, so why go to Gage?"

"I thought he'd understand and he did. But I didn't get up the courage to talk to him until the day we found out you were arrested."

"Fair enough. What did you talk about?"

"Why he was a Daddy and what kinda...Daddy would I need."

"And what did Gage say?"

"A caring one. One who'd respect my limits and who could help me mend what was broken."

"How are you broken, baby boy?"

"Someone hurt me." He flinched as Raul's fingers dug painfully into his thighs. "He said if I voiced it, then it no longer had power."

Raul stared into his eyes and then Raul was brushing his fingertips down over Pure's eyes closing them. Not being able to see the other man's expression helped ease the anxiety that was building. Voice it, that's all he had to do. It was three words, but they held so much power to bring forth memories of that night. Raul's arms came around him, and he tucked his face into the curve of Raul's neck.

"Just say it, baby."

He hugged Raul tight and tried to push the words past the knot forming in his throat. "I was asked on a date by the popular boy. He didn't take no for an answer. He was raping me when the owner of the property interrupted. I said no so many times." He held Raul tighter as he felt the tears slip from beneath his lowered lids.

Raul gently stroked his back, and the leaner man's body pushed deeper between his thighs. "What was his name?"

He couldn't help his smile at the sexy growling order, and he shook his head. He tried to hold onto Raul as the man pulled away and he earned a stubborn glare. It hadn't turned out as painful as he'd assumed. It wasn't easier to admit because he refused to see himself as that naive boy with his childish crush. He knew saying it out loud was one thing, allowing himself to be physically vulnerable with someone was another matter he'd have to work through later.

"You don't tell Daddy no when it comes to this. I'm promising spankings now and not just threatening."

"Last time I checked, he was serving a minimum of twenty-five."

"What prison? I'll request it when I turn myself in."

"You're not turning yourself in. My plan was flawless." He started to jump down from the bench and Raul grabbed him to hold him in place.

"Boy, I will do whatever to protect you just like you did with me. I trust you and the team to get me out. I can watch my back until then."

"Bullshit!"

"Boy, don't test me."

Strong hands shoved down the back of his sweatpants and gripped his cheeks in a punishing grip.

"You will learn that your safety and happiness is always above mine. You will do as I say. I can't do what I need to do if I don't know you're outside watching my back. Understand that. Who else would go above and beyond for me?"

He could only nod, he didn't agree, but he also never thought he'd feel as if he couldn't trust his Trenton team. They'd become his family, all the Crews stood together no matter what came at them, and then they threw Raul under the bus. The wait and see option was bullshit, and he wasn't going to stand for it.

He gasped as the tight hold eased and his hips were pulled closer to the edge of the bench. Pleasure caused goosebumps to spread over his skin. He groaned as he pushed his lips to Raul's, and he felt free as the man took over the kiss. He started to protest as Raul retreated, but then his shirt and Raul's hit the floor. His inexperience embarrassed him as he shivered, and his cock tented the front of his sweatpants with just a few kisses and touches.

"Fuck, boy, you made Daddy wait too fucking long."

Cool air touched his cock as the fabric disappeared, and a rough hand circled his length. He leaned back to rest his weight on his hands as biting kisses teased his chest and over his stomach, then a door slammed.

"Boys, unless I see rings you two ain't banging in my house."

"Shit," Raul groaned and leaned his forehead on Pure's chest. "That was a hard-on killer."

He couldn't decide if he wanted to scream in frustration or die of mortification, but in the end, figured it was better to deflect. "We need to get going anyway." He began to ease off the bench only to be stopped by Raul pinching his chin and forcing their gazes to meet.

"This isn't over, boy. We still need to have a Daddy and boy conversation. Also, I want an uninterrupted kiss."

"Okay."

"Okay, what?"

"Okay...Daddy."

"I've gotten off so many times imagining you calling me that."

He didn't know what to say. All of this was too new, and he needed space to process, but in less than an hour, they'd be alone in the safehouse with a whole new relationship to figure out.

WHAT NOW?

*H*e watched Pure from the front window of the empty house as he signed for the renovation supplies and showed the guys where to off-load them. He glared as one of them checked out his boy's ass when Pure turned to return to the house. The possessiveness and jealousy still weren't getting any easier and now that he knew what his boy felt like—the taste of him—it was even harder to deal.

He strode through the house. It was a beautiful, older home perfect for a small family, but it was looking a bit worn down. Pure had told him that the family had lived there for several years. He peered out the glass in the kitchen door and growled as his boy stripped off the sleeveless t-shirt. He traced the soft curve of Pure's belly and lower to the baggy jeans that hung low on his hips.

The night they'd arrived, they'd rolled out sleeping bags on the living room floor. He'd had his close to Pure, but he had so much to think about he hadn't held his boy like he'd craved. Pure was reserved and untouched in a healthy way. The thought of someone hurting Pure when he was so young threw him into a rage. It wasn't enough the fucker was locked up. He hadn't joked when he said he'd request the same prison. He was in danger of going down for murder now.

A phone beeping caught his attention, and he turned to find Pure's on the kitchen counter. He stretched out his arm to grab it and saw there were several messages. He put in Pure's code, and the phone started beeping constantly.

Gage: Pure, boy, you better check-in.

Little: Check the info.

Linus: I'm kicking your oversized fucking ass.

Peaches: You're not helping him Pure. Call me.

Liv: Hey, man, you're set.

Linus: You don't call in now you're off the fucking team.

It was message after message of threats, and there were a few numbers and names he didn't know. Several with coded messages or just a string of numbers like passcodes. What was the boy playing at?

A loud beeping reached him, and he looked outside again to see a delivery man approaching Pure. He reached for his weapon and waited as Pure signed for a package, then the stranger left. Pure closed the garage door, and Raul put the phone back to sleep, returning it to its spot on the counter.

"This is what I was waiting for."

"What is it?" he asked.

"Information. All the files are encoded and one wrong password and the hard drive fries itself."

He watched as Pure opened the box and pulled out a laptop wrapped in bubble wrap. Raul took a seat at the table on the single chair and pulled his boy down on his thigh, but not before Pure made a grab for his phone. There was a list of files, each one was protected, and Pure entered the code for the first one.

He twined his arms around Pure's waist and enjoyed the feel of his warm, hair-roughened skin on his exposed forearms. It was only a matter of time before Pure was ripped from him. He wasn't holding his breath that he'd remain free. His brave front was just that, a front, to make his boy feel better, but he was going to need to make his boy feel safe. Touch and kiss him, memorize it for the long years ahead. He trusted the team, still had hope that they were doing everything to find out who wanted to take him down.

"You do know the team is trying to get ahold of you, right?"

"I quit."

"You what?"

"When they wouldn't fight for you, I quit. If they ain't going to back one of us up then when are they going to toss the rest of us onto the rails? I can't trust them, and I said so."

Pure lived for his job. They were family and always had been, but his boy had pretty much told them all to fuck off. His boy had given up his life for him and possibly his freedom. He raised his hand to turn Pure's head slightly to reach his perfect lips. He tilted his head just until he captured Pure's mouth. He sunk his fingers into Pure's soft hair and the kiss turned rough, their labored breaths harsh. Raul moaned and parted his lips just enough to tease Pure's tongue with the tip of his. Fuck, just kissing his boy made him hard—made him forget the outside world. He'd known it would, but the intensity of it shocked him.

He gave Pure softer kisses as he spoke. "Baby, you love your job, and Linus said he was going to fire you."

"I figured you'd check my messages sooner rather than later. Linus doesn't like that it wasn't his decision."

"What did Liv mean by you're all set?"

"Next safehouse."

"So you're in contact with at least—"

"No, Liv and I broke radio contact days ago. No one knows where I am. The laptop was sent by an old friend who owed me one. The one who found out about the bounty."

Breaking all contact and quitting was putting distance between Pure and the operation, but that didn't mean his boy was in the clear. He wasn't comfortable with the plan.

"What are we looking at?"

"I had my friend track the IP addresses from the original request, and it bounced all over hell and back, but it appears to be coming from a small town on the Texas/Mexico border. There's rumors of a cartel running operations out of there, but no one traces back to you. At least not yet."

His eyes scanned docs one after another, and he recognized names but no one he ever came into direct contact with.

"We're running traces on known associates and seeing if they align with any of your recent bounties, but it'll take a while to make it through all the channels."

"What does your gut say?"

"It's about more than a bounty. Someone has that kinda money...they can pay off whoever they want. This is personal. It isn't just about killing you. It's about making you suffer first. That's a hatred borne of more than you picked the wrong flyer off the wall."

"It does seem rather extreme. I've had threats, a few have even thrown a few shots, but it's never anything this intense."

That's what bothered him. Criminals knew that if they ran, they were going down unless they had the funds to make it to a nice non-extradition country to chill out the rest of their lives. The people who hit the board at Trenton or even his radar when he was freelance weren't in the range of throwing out six-figure bounties on his head.

He grinned as his boy's belly started growling. "Does my boy need food?" He loved making the big man blush.

He eased Pure off his lap, and when his boy tried to move away, he turned him until Pure straddled his thighs. Pure held himself stiffly.

"Boy, come closer to Daddy," he ordered and deeply groaned as his boy wiggled on his lap until their chests were flush. The soft hair tickled his smooth chest. He wanted a distraction for both of them. "Do you think about Daddy loving on you?"

"Yes."

"Yes, what?"

"Daddy." Pure's voice was so shy and soft. His innocence was sexy. It always had been. In his dreams, it had always been him teaching his boy—making sure his touch was the only one Pure would ever experience. He didn't care about the time before, that was violence, and all he wanted was to love on his boy.

"Tonight, I want you to sleep beside me. In my arms and nowhere else, do you understand?"

Pure shyly nodded, and Raul gave his boy a tender kiss.

"Now, I'm going to feed you while you work."

He helped Pure off his lap and reseated him in the chair. Jenn had stocked them with groceries and a few kitchen essentials. While he moved around the kitchen, he caught his boy tracking his movements. Later they would talk about expectations and his boy's limitations, he was going to enjoy the time they had while he could. He wanted to learn everything about his boy and let his boy know that being loved on had nothing to do with pain or humiliation.

COULD PURE DO THIS?

*T*he later it became, the more he tried to put off going to bed. They'd kissed and touched, he knew the feel of Raul's rough hand around his length, but he'd been careful about initiating too much intimacy. He was still scared of sex. Worried if it would hurt. Masturbation felt good, and his fantasies were embarrassing. The scenes he watched with the spankings and bondage, they made him feel funny.

He pretended everything was normal as he walked out of the steamy bathroom with a towel around his hips. Drying his hair with a second one, he paused as he entered the living room to find one of the air mattresses made up with their sleeping bags and blankets. A fire was burning in the stone fireplace.

Raul had showered before him and was standing next to the bed they were going to share. Baggy pajama bottoms hung low on Raul's hips. He traced the thin line of black hair that ran from his outie navel then fanned out where it met thick, tight curls. He felt the only thing keeping the pants up was the bulge under the dark cotton.

He fisted his hands in the towel and tried to swallow down the lump in his throat.

"Boy, use your words."

Gage said he needed to trust Raul. That a boy or sub's greatest gift to their Dom or Daddy was unquestionable trust. He didn't know if he had in him. But he had to take a leap of faith. "I'm nervous."

"I am too."

"Why?"

"Because for years, I've looked at you like the sun, bright and beautiful, light, and I felt so unworthy."

"I thought Daddies were supposed to be confident."

"I think it's better to be honest. The whole time I've known you, you were waiting for the one. The happily ever after and kids, I've never done a permanent thing in my life. I don't know what happens tomorrow. Jail or we beat the odds for another twenty-four—"

He was about to protest, but a single glare from Raul made him rethink that.

"No, we're going to be honest with each other. If it's between you or me, it's always going to be your safety first. You know that."

He did. When Raul acted as his spotter, they were in sync—trusting each other to know when was enough. He never argued with Raul over that. Raul slowly approached him, their gazes were locked, and it took everything in him to stand his ground. The spicy scent that was all Raul overwhelmed him.

"Since the moment I met you, everyone else paled in comparison."

He allowed the man to remove the damp towel from his clenched fists. He had to slightly lower his gaze to meet Raul's. His broader and softer form always made him compare himself to the leaner, more muscular Raul. His light brown skin was smooth to his hairier frame.

"My boy is so beautiful."

He wanted to protest but whatever argument he'd tried to

come up with ended as Raul tugged the fluffy towel from around his hips.

"Raul." His voice was barely above a whisper.

"It's okay, boy, Daddy's here to take care of you."

Callous roughened hands gripped his hips gently, and he didn't think twice about following the shorter man's lead. He didn't break eye contact even when Raul lowered to the air mattress, bringing him down too.

"Lie down, baby."

He stretched out, feeling too exposed and unsure of what happened next. He waited for something, maybe Raul to push his limits too soon. Yet, that isn't what happened. Raul remained sitting on the edge of the bed. Fingertips gently traced the angles of his face and followed the curves of his lips. He felt them tremble. And he held his breath when Raul stretched his right arm across Pure's body, and the knuckles on Raul's left hand rubbed his bearded cheek.

"Have you ever thought of me when you get yourself off?"

He waited to feel trapped beneath the other man's weight. Instead, Raul simply bracketed his upper body and his smooth chest barely touching his.

"Y—yes."

"How long, baby boy?"

"Too long."

"Do you play with your tight hole when you do?"

"It scares me."

"Boy, there is nothing to be frightened of with me."

"There's everything to be frightened of with you. You're the only one with the power to hurt me."

"Baby boy." Raul's voice lowered as the man brushed his lips to Pure's. "I can't promise that I won't hurt you in some way, but it'll never be intentional."

He almost grabbed Raul when the man pushed to his feet and loomed at the side of their bed. Curbing the urge to cover himself was the hardest of his life. He hadn't been naked with another person in his life. Even when he was in the service, he'd timed his showers to where he'd be alone.

"Has anyone ever seen you like this, boy?" The question was barely more than a dangerous growl.

"No, Daddy." He nibbled at his lower lip, and he froze with the plump lower curve between his teeth. Raul stripped his pants down his legs, A thick, long cock and heavy sac came into view, then muscular thighs covered with tight, dark curls.

He was lost as to what to do, and a shiver rolled through him from head to toe—a strange tightening beneath his skin. Raul didn't say a word as the man laid down on the bed. The man who wanted to be his Daddy slipped his forearm beneath his neck.

"We don't have to do anything, boy, this is about you getting used to trusting your Daddy."

Raul rested his right arm over him, palmed his hip, and then Raul's mouth took his in the softest kiss. No tongue or heat, just gentle nips and he felt his body respond to the tender caresses— the press of Raul's hard, leaner body. Raul's hard cock pressing into his hip. But Raul didn't rut or try to speed up the seduction.

Raul was warm and strong. Pure felt awkward as he shifted until he could slip his right arm under Raul's side. His left hand shook as he splayed his hand and fingers to the center of Raul's chest. The kiss ended to allow them to catch their breath, and Raul rested their foreheads together. Their mingled breath was teasing each other's mouths.

"Tell Daddy what you imagined him doing to you."

It was a softly issued order. Everything about this felt odd, from the caring of the normally gruff man and the soft crackling of the fire. Raul's fingers tightened on his hip. He watched the man's expression in the light of the flames. The slight trembling of his body increased at the stroking of Raul's hand from his hip, under him to the curve of his ass cheek. Raul gave it a soft squeeze and then moved lower along his thigh.

He gasped as Raul's hand slipped between his legs and Raul unhurriedly parted his thighs. Opening him wide, and he felt his face starting to heat.

"You feel so much better than I imagined, boy."

Raul's darker skin was a striking contrast to his pale, hairy thighs.

"I just want you to lie back and let Daddy take care of you."

He almost grabbed Raul to keep the man close but resisted as Raul scooted down the bed, lying on his stomach between Pure's legs. Firm lips mouthed his sac, and he let out the most unmanly squeak. He couldn't take his gaze from Raul, and it seemed as if he had the same problem, Raul focused on him. He knew in his gut that Raul was waiting for any sign of distress.

Raul's arms were wrapped around his thick thighs. Strong hands and fingers cushioned by the softness of his belly. He was caught somewhere between lust and panic, gentleness and a need for more. His body no longer his own, possessed by Raul to do with as he pleased. Yet, the fear still outweighed the lust. There was a tightrope of anticipation of when he would lose that edge of awakening pleasure from Raul's caring and attention.

He bent his knees slightly at the slow flick of Raul's tongue along his perineum. He felt the rush of Raul's hot, wet breath, and then it happened, that first tentative lick brought the nightmares to blaring reality. He seized Raul's wrists in a grip tight enough to make his hands ache.

As the hated tears filled his eyes, Raul's body blanketed his, knees on either side of his thighs.

"Baby boy, look at me."

He shook his head, not wanting to see disappointment, and he crossed his arms over his chest. Hugging himself in that old way of self-soothing.

"Nicolas, you will open your eyes and look at me. Now."

The edge and harshness of Raul's tone made him slowly open his eyes. The soft smile that gently curved Raul's lips and the tender stroke of fingertips along his bearded jaw eased some of the tension.

"There's Daddy's baby boy. You never have to be ashamed of your fear—your limits."

Raul slipped to the side to press fully to him. His Daddy's touch turned soothing as Raul eased him down from the abrupt anxiety attack.

"Now, boy." As Raul spoke, Pure's legs were parted, and the left one was draped over Raul's thigh. "Daddy wants a kiss."

He tipped his chin and Raul took his mouth in a deep, slow kiss and he shook at the first touch of their tongues. He wrapped his arms around Raul's neck, and then he lightly bit his Daddy's tongue at the stroke of rough fingertips around his hole. There wasn't a rush, Raul didn't try to push inside, and then Raul cupped his balls. He gasped at the slow roll then the sound morphed into a moan as Raul took his cock in hand. His body jerked with each stroke.

Between kisses, Raul whispered how good Daddy's boy was. It was frustratingly slow. He didn't even protest when Raul returned to his spot straddling his thighs.

"Daddy…" Raul's new title broke as it passed his lips. Raul's features were harsher, his breaths hot where Raul had his mouth just resting on his.

"That's right, baby boy, just keep your eyes on me," Raul whispered, then lifted to sit back on his heels. Adjusting until the fat head of his cock was pressed to Pure's hole. "You're gonna come for Daddy, and then I want to coat your tight little hole with cum. Daddy won't do it inside. Can you do that for me?"

He nodded fast as he shoved his arms underneath his pillow and crossed them. He was spread wide for Raul. Vulnerable yet safe, he looked down the length of his body to find Raul stroking their cocks in tandem. Raul was watching too. Sweat beaded his skin, and his hips started to roll up and down, fucking in and out of Raul's fist. He barely paid attention to the danger of Raul's thick dick at his hole.

"Fuck, baby boy, so sexy."

He threw his head back as his sac drew up and fire roared through his veins, and then his belly was covered in his release.

"Suck Daddy's fingers clean."

He barely had time to open his mouth before Raul gave him his seed-covered hand. The more he sucked, the more brutal Raul jacked his cock. He licked every drop from Raul's hand and fingers. He choked once and twice as Raul's middle and index checked his gag reflex. The pressure of the flared head starting to push inside bordered on pain, but as he protested, Raul cursed, and wetness spread over his hole and balls.

"Goddamn, boy, you made Daddy come so hard."

He quickly wrapped his arms around Raul's waist when the man rested his weight on him. The kiss they shared was erotic and lazy, no rush to separate.

"Did Daddy make you feel good?"

"Yes, Daddy." Raul rutted his spent cock against his balls.

"I'm going to go get a rag to clean us up and then we're going to bed. You have a lot to do tomorrow."

"Yes, Daddy."

He didn't know what else to say when Raul gave him one more kiss and then got out of bed. He laid there analyzing what happened. Raul could've taken him, forced him to submit to a fucking, but he hadn't. He reached between his legs and gathered Raul's release and then brought his hand to his mouth. He tasted Raul, it was different from his own, and he closed his eyes as he imagined sucking the thick length. Tasting Raul as his Daddy came in his mouth instead of on his skin. Fantasy was all well and good, but what happened when reality didn't live up to what he imagined? What would happen if he was still afraid?

THEIR TIME WAS QUICKLY COMING TO AN END

$\mathcal{R}$aul savored the few nights of sleeping with his boy held tight in his arms. The tentative touches and handjobs, but he knew their time was coming to an end. Every day that passed was another one where the authorities would find them and not just he would go to jail. He couldn't allow his baby boy to get caught. He could do his time, even die as long as it meant that Pure was free to live.

Always on the run, looking over their shoulders, that wasn't the life he'd pictured with Pure. Nicolas deserved so much more. Pure deserved the husband and kids, a house filled with laughter and love. What the fuck could he contribute to that? Nothing.

He could picture it though. When he was at his lowest remembering the way Pure had looked cooking breakfast for the Crew kids, and it had been amazing. A life he hadn't thought he would have before. Not that he could. He'd played the hand he was dealt and lost.

He shifted on the air mattress and stared up at the ceiling as he listened to Pure make the final repairs to the outside of the house. Since he'd had to stay out of sight, he'd taken over the painting and repairs inside.

The sound of an engine approaching had him rolling to his feet and silently making it to the kitchen door. He peeked through the curtains, and a big cop was approaching Pure where his boy was standing just inside the garage.

"Nicolas."

"Officer Daniels, what sin did I commit to deserve a visit from you?"

He felt his brows draw together at the obvious hatred in his boy's tone. He couldn't miss the way the cop's hand was resting on his sidearm. The tension amped up, as much as he knew his boy was capable of taking care of himself that didn't mean he wasn't prepared to step in.

"Do you know the whereabouts of Raul Martinez?"

"Nope. If you checked with your sources, you'd know I no longer work for Trenton Security. What happens with them isn't my business anymore."

His entire body went on high alert as the man approached his boy. Pure stood his ground. He wrapped his hand around the doorknob, ready to open and rush outside.

"You looking for another broken jaw, Daniels?"

"Nicolas, we both know you were just playing hard to get. You're not as innocent as you want to pretend."

"Badge or not, this time I'll make sure you lose those teeth."

Everything slowed down as the cop raised his hand to place it on Pure's chest. One second he was on his feet, and the next, Pure had the man on the ground with his arm twisted behind his back.

"Arrest me or get the fuck off my property."

Pure released the man's wrist and put distance between them waiting for the man to attack. The big cop was instantly on his feet, but he didn't go to restrain Pure or arrest him.

"This isn't the end. You don't have those thugs watching your back anymore. Welcome home, Nicolas."

Raul remained battle-ready until he heard the engine start and the car spun its tires backing out of the driveway. He didn't care if the coast was clear or not, he threw open the door, and Pure was instantly in his arms.

"Boy, it's okay. I should've—"

Pure held him tight enough that it was hard to breathe. "No, you shouldn't have. We have to get moving. Grab our go-bag… everything else is already at the next location."

He tried to hold on as Pure pulled away. He wanted to demand answers, but Pure was already on the move, and he followed Pure into the house. So many questions remained unanswered. Who the cop was, and why did the stranger make Pure lose his calm? Pure had told him the bastard who assaulted him was in jail.

He rushed inside to get ready for when it was time to move out. Several minutes passed and they had everything ready, and the sound of the deep growl of a motorcycle filled the house.

"Mom's here."

He kept close to Pure, and if the moment wasn't tense, he'd have laughed at the tiny woman straddling a huge bike in her flowery little sundress. She removed her helmet, and her mouth was pulled into a huge grin. He didn't even know how she maneuvered the damn thing.

"I so need to get me one of these." She knocked the kickstand down and dismounted.

"Maybe for your birthday."

"You promise that every year. I'm just going to keep yours." She pouted as they exchanged keys and he frowned as Pure handed over his cellphone.

Pure got to work strapping their pack to the back of the bike.

"Here's five hundred in cash and there's another thousand on a prepaid card. This arrived a few days ago, new IDs and passports just in case. There's also a burner phone for emergencies."

He took the envelope and slipped it into the inside pocket of his leather jacket. "You're doing too much, Jenn."

"For my boy, it's never too much. Just keep him safe. I checked the bike for tracking devices just in case, and everything is in the clear. Also, the bike has a full tank, so it should get you to the next safehouse. I don't know where and I don't want to."

Goodbyes were exchanged, and she held onto Pure for long minutes while they had a private conversation. When she backed up, he saw the tears on her cheeks.

"Wear your vest. I don't want you in my ER."

"I promise."

"I'm gonna clean the house and make sure nothing of y'all's is left. Call when you can."

He'd normally be the one in front, but he mounted after Pure. They both slipped on their helmets, then the bike rumbled to life and they roared out onto the main road. He didn't like not knowing where they were heading, but he trusted Pure. There weren't many people he did, and Pure was putting his life and freedom on the line. Soon he was going to have to do something about that.

He followed Pure's lead as they sped through traffic and finally made it to the highway. They were headed north, and he had a bad feeling about where they were headed. He didn't trust those two fuckers farther than he could throw them. Freddie and Horace offered assistance if it benefited them in some way. They were feral woodsmen who lived by no code but their own.

The Trenton Crew trusted them, and he'd worked with them on a few operations. He'd have to keep a closer eye on Pure. Freddie and Horace tended to try to get pretty men back to their tents. Pure wasn't going to be one of them.

He hugged Pure's waist tighter as time passed slowly and they drew nearer to the cutoff they needed to make to the unmarked trail to hike into the camp. He wished Pure's heavy jacket wasn't in the way. This was what he'd miss the most when he was locked up. The freedom that came too late to touch his boy. Claim him and have his boy call him Daddy. He should stop the progression now, to leave Pure to find someone worthier of his first time, but he was too selfish for it.

His boy's pleasure—first time—belonged to no one but him. He craved to own his boy's sexual awakening. Pure's trust was his greatest gift. Something he'd always treasure. The only thing he could ask would be that Pure moved on and found the happiness his boy deserved. For Pure to have all his dreams come true, and until he had to let go to save his boy, he'd take everything that was his.

SETTING UP THE PERIMETER

*E*very muscle in his body was tense. The farther away they rode, didn't make him feel any safer. He wouldn't completely relax until they made it to the camp. The gravel shifted under the wheels of his bike as he took the unmarked narrow path. Unless someone was familiar with it, anyone would easily miss the turn. He knew the spot where he was supposed to meet Horace and Freddie. He hadn't seen them since the last time he escaped for a week of camping.

As much as he wanted to get off the bike, Raul was the only thing keeping him together. Not only had he felt his world falling apart when the cruiser pulled into the driveway, but then his knees almost gave out when he'd seen the uniformed officer getting out of the car. He'd left Atlanta to go home to Powers to avoid his past that seemed to have followed him from his last tour. Daniels hadn't taken no for an answer. He'd never pretended he was in the closet. He'd just been another *fag* asking for it.

He hadn't been able to get stateside fast enough. He was strong and never let the cracks show, but the sight of Daniels had made him physically ill. His no sex rule was an irresistible challenge. No seemed to elicit the response of a hunter with their prey in the crosshairs. Avoiding kisses or touches to some men was a signal just to try harder. He wasn't prey or an elusive target. He wouldn't stand still and submit, never again would he be vulnerable—he'd take the kill shot. Consequences didn't matter.

He almost noticed the hidden trail too late. An involuntary smile tugged at his mouth as he felt a growl against his back as he shot between two trees. He rolled to a stop over the uneven ground. As soon as he kicked down the stand, Raul was dismounting and jerking his helmet off.

"Boy, who taught your ass to drive?"

"Daddy, um, I think I handled the dirt bike and my motorcycle just fine."

"Don't Daddy me, Baby boy."

He hid his amusement as he found the pack his two friends left him and shook out a camouflage cover and hid his bike away.

"Ignoring me isn't going to save your ass later."

"Now, Pure, I didn't think that was your thing."

A gravelly amused voice had him pulling his forty-five from his holster. Horace stepped forward with his hands up with Freddie aiming a twelve-gauge over the man's shoulder.

"Horace, always a delight." He put his weapon away and went to grab their pack, but Raul got to it first.

"Yeah, we hear that a lot," Freddie replied, as he rolled his ice-blue eyes and lowered his weapon.

Freddie moved from behind Horace. Freddie watched them coolly and dragged his thick fingers through his heavily silver-streaked long hair. Tattoos covered every inch of exposed skin. The only thing ink-free were the two men's faces, but the numerous scars rose thick from their cheeks, lips, and foreheads.

"The hot twins airdropped a bag for you last night. Our camp never gets this much excitement until Liv and his pretty-boy come to visit." Freddie's smirk was disturbing.

It was well known that Liv and Fielding went camping a few times a year, and his friends gave the recluses a show for their shared kinks.

"And I don't need details."

Yes, they made him uncomfortable most of the time, but after he needed some time away, he'd visited the two men. They were foster brothers, but other than that they didn't talk much about the past. They could sit together with their shoulders touching and never say a word. It was as if they shared this mental connection. Automatically filling the other's needs, a refill of coffee or a plate. He wouldn't say that when the two men went to their tents that he didn't have to take a walk. To be so isolated, having only the other for company, and hearing them pleasure themselves in their neighboring tents was embarrassing.

"Come on, we have a three-mile hike, and there's rain coming." Horace didn't wait to see if they followed.

Everyone lapsed into silence for the start of the hike. He jumped slightly as Raul took his hand, lacing their fingers together. He turned to find Raul smiling at him and heat infused his cheeks when Raul lifted their hands to his mouth, brushing his lips to Pure's knuckles.

"You come out here a lot?"

He didn't miss the edge to Raul's voice.

"No, maybe once a year or twice for the last four. No one is crazy enough to come into the woods knowing they live out here. They're slowly building a cabin, I doubt they'll ever finish it, but I help while I'm out here. It's just something to keep them busy."

"Have they ever touched you?"

"We don't touch other people's property without permission," Freddie growled.

"I'm not property," he protested, but only received twin grunts in reply.

"No, we all have our own tents. They keep my gear safe, so my tent and bag are already there. Sin and Saint were supposed to drop your supplies and a few special requests for me."

"Sin and Saint?"

He hadn't wanted to involve the Sheriff's boys, but he hadn't completely cut off ties. The Crew partners were bratty, and he needed a few allies.

"Pelter know?"

"Yes."

"What the fuck, Pure?"

"He fought for you as much as he could, harder than the Trenton guys. He gave me all the information...called me when the transport left."

"He could lose his job."

"No, Horace and Freddie or Mom have been passing notes and taking them to Twitch. He sends them along, and Pelter destroys them after reading them. No electronic footprint. Everything I've purchased has been in cash. Weapons have all been bought from a dealer I know from the streets from my days with SWAT."

He felt Raul's disappointment in the way the man became quiet. Raul hated when he took risks. Before the shift in their relationship, he sensed that Raul was going to have a lot more to say about what he did. He'd survived long before Raul came into his life. His wounds had festered and scarred over, but he'd survived just fine.

The scents of a campfire reached him long before they arrived at the camp. There was a small clearing big enough for the small, rustic cabin and the camp situated at the base of the steps that led up to a big porch. Raul hadn't said a word for an hour as they pitched his tent, placed their gear, pads and sleeping bags inside. Horace was working on dinner, and Freddie had taken off toward the lake for a bath.

Raul set up two camp chairs opposite the fire from Horace and Freddie's. He smiled his thanks to Horace as the man tapped a metal bucket filled with warmed water for him to clean up. Horace nodded toward the sheet that was strung up from the porch for his privacy. He knew the man did it on purpose. They might be crazy, but they knew about pain and scars.

He dug out a change of clothes, a towel, and the biodegradable bar for hair, body, and shaving. The sun was just starting to set, but there was still plenty of light for him to wash by. He used the towel to grab the handle of the bucket and carried it to his private area. He stopped on the rubber mat and placed the bucket on the edge. Then he grabbed the metal cup where it was hung on one of the porches supports.

It didn't take him long to get everything set up and started to strip his shoes and socks, but he froze as Raul joined him. He tried to even out his breathing as he waited for a fight—yet it didn't come. He was in Raul's arms, and the man held him tight as he captured his lips in a rough kiss. Strong hands were painfully fisting in his hair.

This wasn't the gentle teasing ones Raul gave him since their first. Teeth sharply nipped his bottom lip, and Raul was removing his clothes without care. He didn't even fight him. His cock was hard and aching. Every time he reached for Raul, his hands were pushed away and then his back hit the unfinished wall. He bit his lip to suppress his shocked yelp as Raul swallowed his length.

He looked down at Raul. The man was bobbing and softly groaning, then Raul dug his fingertips into his ass cheeks. He tipped his head back, crossed his arms over his face, and sunk his teeth into his forearm. He fucked Raul's mouth and rose on his toes when Raul sucked hard when he tried to retreat. One minute he was on the verge of coming, then he was turned, and Raul's face was buried between his cheeks. His nails clawed at the wood as he pressed his cheek to it.

He quickly grabbed Raul's thick hair, and it was getting harder to keep quiet. Raul knew just how to play with his hole to make sure he didn't panic. He thrust backward as he felt the push of Raul's tongue, felt the pressure. When he would have begged for more, Raul was on his feet and pressed to his back.

"Baby boy"—Raul nipped his earlobe—"you almost made Daddy come too soon. You want to fuck Daddy, don't you?"

If he was supposed to talk, it wasn't going to happen, so he just nodded.

"I bet that thick cock would tear Daddy's ass up."

He froze, not believing what he heard.

"Daddy likes to be fucked, but I also know what my boy needs. You want to suck Daddy's cock and play with his ass."

He didn't answer just turned then moved Raul. His hands shook as he removed Raul's t-shirt, dropping it to rest on top of his clothes. He undid Raul's jeans as he kissed the side of Raul's throat, moving lower. His Daddy's skin was hot and smooth, and then he was on his knees. He finished undressing Raul. He tipped his head back, and Raul's fingers combed through his hair. He opened his mouth as his Daddy painted his lips with pre-cum. He sucked too hard and triggered his gag reflex.

"Easy, baby boy, good boys need to practice on Daddy first." Raul wrapped his hand around all but a few inches. "Now, suck Daddy."

He did, and it was odd. Raul had never asked him to give him a blowjob. The ring of Raul's fingers and thumb stopped him, he curved his tongue beneath and pushed the head to the roof of his mouth. The loose foreskin teased his tongue as he sucked in a slow rhythm learning the feel and taste of Raul. Raul teased the corner of his mouth.

"My boy looks so pretty sucking Daddy's cock."

Slowly he realized that his Daddy was letting him take more, but just enough that he could bob along the length. He whimpered as he rolled the foreskin over the fat head and nibbled before sucking Raul in again.

"Shit, baby boy, that's right."

He drew his gaze upward to find Raul watching him with a

look in his eyes he'd never seen before. It was soft, almost what he thought love would look like. He wanted to taste Raul, give the man pleasure. He wanted the moments where the outside wouldn't intrude—reality wouldn't take away what he'd just learned to accept. As he tightly gripped Raul's ass cheeks, he started moving faster, increasing the pressure, and savoring every growl from above him.

Raul's hand sunk deeper into his hair, twisting it around his fingers, and he took advantage. He ignored his gag reflex, the slight edge of awkwardness, and brought his hand to his cock. Jacking the length quickly as he played with Raul's hole with the other. The hair tickled his fingers. Raul cursed and groaned. All the things he dreamed were coming true. He jerked off faster, and just as he came, Raul's release filled his mouth. He swallowed greedily. Raul's upper body leaned forward, and his Daddy hugged his head.

"God, baby boy. Shit, you made Daddy come too fast."

He eased away as Raul straightened. He met his Daddy's heavy-lidded eyes.

"Was I a good boy, Daddy?"

"The best."

Raul knelt until they could kiss. His Daddy's rough hands caressed his back, and too soon the kiss ended, but Raul didn't just walk away. He stood there as Raul washed him tenderly from head to toe. Praising him with each caress and stolen kiss. He might not admit it out loud, but he knew their time was coming to an end. That memories were going to be all he had, but he'd rather have memories of being loved on—of being fulfilled—than nothing at all.

AN ENDLESS WHODUNIT

*H*e could almost forget the clanging of a jail cell door was waiting to close behind him. The quiet of the woods allowed him to hear steps in any direction. Silence of forest animals hiding from danger like an alarm system. His boy was off with Freddie gathering firewood, and he was staring across the fire pit at Horace.

Horace's curly black hair was cut short and was streaked with the littlest of silver. He was shirtless and excessively hairy, with partial sleeves of bloody and white skulls from his wrists up. If he wasn't mistaken, there were a few new skulls since the last time he'd worked with the man.

"You taking care of Pure?"

He felt his brow furrow, and he frowned at the guttural voice. "What business is it of yours?"

"More than you think. We've been watching him a lot longer than you have."

"He's mine."

"Ain't saying he isn't, he's a good kid. Vicious and deadly, but sweet. He deserves a man who isn't going to rot in jail or have a needle stuck in his arm."

"I didn't ask for him to break me out."

"You don't leave a man behind, especially someone who's watched your back...kept your ass alive. Who have you fucked over so bad that they'd go to all the trouble to set you up? Ya' see, the way I figure it, whoever is after your ass is already locked up and wants to take care of the job personally. And has the funds to slap down a six-figure price tag on your back."

"Do you know how many people I've earned a bounty on?"

He'd been doing this most of his life, what else did he have? He'd been shot at, shot, stabbed, and one guy had tried to run him down with a semi. It wasn't like he had a lot of friends. Never once had he thought someone was capable of putting a hit out on him, especially not one that extreme. It was the not knowing that was driving him the craziest.

He wondered if Pure had put himself on the line for the inevitable. He didn't believe he was going to survive the outcome, and he hated the thought of leaving his boy behind. It was purely selfish. He didn't want to think of another man touching—loving on—his boy, making all his dreams come true. That should be his job.

"Just has to be one, man. Some man lost his old lady because he went to jail. Casualty during the operation. Lots of reasons a man would want another dead. Sometimes it could be a man just breathed wrong."

"How have you stayed out of jail this long?"

"Peaches is the best at her job."

The casualness of Horace's answer shouldn't shock him, but it did. There was something dead in the man's eyes, same with Freddie. They carried themselves like feral beasts going to war at any moment—just the span of a breath separated them from doing the unthinkable without regret or mercy. As they were no longer a part of society, they saw no reason to adhere to the rules. Even if they lived within the town limits, he couldn't see them abiding by the laws of civilization. To them, murder was nothing more than the response to a threat. Old ways from ancient times where it was kill or be killed.

He'd learned that the recluses had been taken down on a double murder charge—a capital offense. Peaches got them off with a technicality. Law was gray. Only as effective as the person who could spin truth into the more beautiful lie.

"And I thought she'd get me out. Pure didn't trust her to do so."

"I wouldn't know, but love makes ya stupid. Makes ya act impulsively. Some would kill for a person to go to these lengths to get them out."

He leaned forward in the chair and rested his elbows on his knees and scrubbed his hands over his face. "I didn't doubt he'd fight for me, but I didn't want him putting his fucking freedom on the line for me. It was my time to do. As long as I knew he was out here, living his life...my stretch would be hard...probably wouldn't survive it but my boy would've had a life. He doesn't deserve to ruin his dreams for me."

"That isn't your choice. He might be your little, but he's also a grown-ass man. With a wicked aim when he has his sniper rifle. We don't know much about Pure's history. Ain't any of our business, but we recognize scars...ones that were put there in cruelty. You don't take the choices of a person like that away. Sometimes it's all we got...the power to decide whether we stand and fight, or we kneel and die."

He jerked his gaze to the left as he heard twigs snap and Pure appeared with his arm full of wood, Freddie not far behind him. His boy was so sweet that when Pure caught him looking, his cheeks above his beard turned scarlet. He looked at Pure's lips and remembered them wrapped around his cock. The way Pure learned how to please his Daddy.

They had called for rain earlier, so the two men piled the

wood on a small platform beside the pit. The covered it with a bright blue tarp. Pure approached him.

"Boy," he said as he tipped his head back.

Pure sweetly smiled with just a hint of shyness as his boy bent down to brush his soft lips to his. Then Pure took the chair next to his. They were both big men, and the one chair wouldn't hold their combined weight. He'd have to wait until they could curl up in their zipped-together sleeping bags later.

"Horace had a theory while you were gone."

"Yeah, what was that?"

"That the person who wants me is on the inside."

"Makes sense that the person would want to take you out themselves. But I hit the county inmate registry...your bounties pulling their time or short-term prisoners doing at most a six-month stint. When I searched State and Federal, it got a bit more complicated. There was about ten names, most of them spend their time in solitary or in closed management. I'm not saying it can't be done. Most men have a price."

He watched as Pure took a bottle from Horace, brought it to his lips and downed a good gulp. He snorted at Pure's hiss. "Horace, you gotta work on that, that shit could strip paint."

"It'a put hair on your chest," Horace grunted, as he hung a pot over the fire he'd just started. He threw in what looked like dried vegetables and meat, filled it with water.

He'd observed the two men closely while he was there. They had a small garden. They hunted. They cut down their own trees to build their home. Neither had a laptop or cellphone, at least no phone he'd seen. If they did, it was only for emergencies. He knew they had supplies brought in once a month for the things they couldn't make.

He grabbed Pure's hand and laced their fingers. He'd never realized the simple intimacy of holding hands or sleeping next to someone was as powerful as it was. And he wanted to take every opportunity.

"You need to draw them out. Like when Liv paraded Fielding down Main Street," Freddie said, then took a swig off the bottle too.

He'd skipped trying it himself. He could use a drink, but he was in the mood to get drunk, and he needed all his senses.

"I'd prefer not to put a bigger target on my boy's back."

"Who said the target would be on his?" Horace asked without looking up from seasoning the soup. "You need to make them fuck up...show their hand. But you take a stand here. Home turf. We have tripwires and sensors all over the place. Nasty little surprises for trespassers. We'd know they were coming from miles away. We got one of the best snipers, tree stand and he can pick them off as we draw them out."

"Why the hell would you two put your asses on the line? What's in it for you?"

"We've been living in these woods since we bought them fifteen years ago. We planned to die out here. Nothing but scattered bones by the time anyone found us. To most, we're just rumors, but to the Crews, Peaches, and Lily, someone might mourn us when we're gone. They will remember we helped protect someone's boy. We're not some record of all the lives we've taken." Horace rubbed his hands over his skull covered arms.

"Pure, you're up." Freddie broke through the momentary silence.

He wondered what was up until he saw Pure rinse his hands in a bucket of water next to the fire pit. He smiled as he watched Pure start to mix up the ingredients for flatbread. Once the dough was done, he used a polished log to pat out each one, then placed it on the hot rocks around the now roaring fire.

All of it was surreal, as if they were just camping with friends and nothing awaited them back in the real world. He didn't miss that Horace suspended another bucket of water over the fire, like the man did it every night for Pure's baths. Maybe he'd taken the men too much at face value. They gave him a lead he hadn't even thought about, but so many names and their time was running out. The whodunit mystery nowhere near being done.

RAUL WAS ACTING STRANGE

othing but the sounds of animals scurrying in the dark and the steady beat of Raul's heart beneath his ear intruded in the interior of their tent. The more they played out all the scenarios, the lists of names whittled down to no one. There had to be something. One enemy that couldn't be excluded without logic. They'd need to move on soon. He didn't know where they'd go, and Horace and Freddie kept telling them to make a stand there.

He awoke that morning to find Raul gone and for several minutes, he'd assumed Raul left. Raul wanted to save him, take him out of the equation, but his one rule he'd followed for over a decade was: no one will ever make him kneel. For days they'd talked and strategized, but they danced all around the issue between him and Raul. He'd analyzed the consequences and accepted them.

When it came to getting passports, he'd spoken with his mom about leaving. As much as it would pain him to leave his mom behind, she'd assured him it wouldn't be a forever goodbye. He rubbed his bearded cheek on Raul's chest.

"Why aren't you asleep, boy?"

"Thinking."

"What are you thinking about?"

"We should head south."

"You mean run."

"Yeah." He turned his head to rest his chin on Raul and met the man's gaze in the dimness. The only light from the fire showing through the tent. "The more we search, the farther we are from the ones responsible. We stay in the US then we'll never be able to breathe."

Raul rubbed the back of his head, gently tugged at his hair, and then slipped his free arm under his head. "That's not the life for you."

"Every morning I wake up, I think you're gone until I hear your voice."

"If I turn myself in, it's the quickest way of finding them. You know that as well as I do."

"I know that."

"Boy, the minute I saw you all those years ago, I wanted you. But after I got to spend time with you, it turned to a craving need. I was so unworthy of it. Never in my life had I met a man who was waiting for his one. So jealous of the man who got you."

Goosebumps broke out over his skin at the tug on his hair.

"Nicolas, you have to let me do what I know is best for you."

He'd closed his eyes at the way Raul whispered his name. When Daddy came to the surface, Raul only called him Nicolas. He'd always hated the name, but when his Daddy used it, it was more an endearment than a curse. "I understand that, but—"

"There's no buts to this. I'll compromise, you have forty-eight hours to come up with a better plan or find the fucker threatening me. After that, I turn myself in, and take my chances."

"What about me?"

"You'll promise to move on. Find that man who will be free for you to call husband and fill a house with all those babies you want. Because as long as you're free to love—to dream, I don't give a fuck what happens to me. Until I take my last breath, Nicolas, your happiness and safety will be my only priority."

The tears dampened his lashes and cheeks. Just as he was about to speak, Raul pushed him to his back.

"Fuck, you don't know how many nights I laid in bed imagining you there. I waited too long to open my mouth and... say something. Now time is running out, but I want to be selfish."

Raul's mouth lowered to his, and he met his Daddy halfway. They both yearned for the same thing. Normalcy and a sense of belonging before the inevitable war. His breathing picked up the pace as the slow hiss of the sleeping bag zipper eased down. He spread his hands over Raul's smooth chest and watched in fascination as his Daddy stripped off his pajama bottoms. He lifted his hips as Raul gripped the sides of his and ever so slowly bared him.

Lingering embarrassment urged him to cover himself, but a deep rumble in his Daddy's chest stopped him. He arched as Raul straddled his upper thighs, their hard cocks aligning.

"Daddy wants you to fuck him. Do you want that, baby boy?"

He was nearly too nervous to speak, but knew his Daddy needed him to use his words. "Yes, Daddy."

He'd always assumed he'd be the one to bottom. Daddy as the top seemed natural, but it wasn't the first time Raul said he wanted to be fucked by his boy. He was terrified if he'd do it right. Raul was always careful not to play with his hole too roughly or push inside. Part of him saw it as a failure—that he wasn't giving his Daddy want he needed.

Raul tugged their pack toward them, and he watched as Raul dug into a side pocket. His Daddy produced a condom and a small bottle of lube.

"I'm nervous." He had to admit it. Raul demanded his honesty.

"There's nothing to be nervous about. Daddy will take care of everything. I've thought about my boy fucking me so many times."

Raul kissed and touched him, nipped sharply at his skin, and he arched into every rough caress. Gasped at the tickle of Raul's long goatee over his ribs. He slammed his eyes shut as his Daddy sucked at the lower curve of his belly, and he bit down on his lip as his Daddy swallowed his length to the back of his throat. The heat and pressure, his Daddy retreated and tongued his slit. His upper body arched forward as he felt his release coming too quickly. He couldn't contain his slutty whimper at the tight ring of his Daddy's fingers at the base of his cock.

He dug his nails into Raul's shoulders as his Daddy sucked his cock faster. Raul growled around his length. Just as he felt he couldn't take anymore, his Daddy released him with a slow retreat. He felt the odd sensation of latex gliding down his cock. His eyes flew open to find his Daddy slicking his fingers and just as Raul moaned, the man slammed his mouth down on his.

Quick biting kisses, teasing of tongues, and his Daddy was stretching himself. He gripped his Daddy's ass and sunk his fingers into Raul's crease. He pulled his Daddy's cheeks wide.

"Fuck, boy, you gonna tear Daddy's ass up," his Daddy whispered.

He didn't have time to respond before Raul shifted, wrapped his hand around his cock, and he brought his hands to his Daddy's hair.

"Daddy's boy is thick, just like I need."

The vice-like grip had him curling his toes. He fisted his hands in the waves of his Daddy's hair. His Daddy started to fuck himself onto his dick. Their mouths pressed together as they each seemed to fight to catch their breath.

"Daddy, may I move?"

"Yes, baby boy."

As soon as he had permission, he bent his knees and planted his feet so he countered his Daddy. Stroked his aching dick repeatedly in Raul's tight ass. The harder he pounded his Daddy, the tighter Raul became.

"Show Daddy how much you love him," Raul demanded and then stilled.

He lost all control. All nervousness fled, and he was fucking his Daddy with no care. It was too much and not enough. His muscles strained, and his thighs burned. But the second Raul's calloused hand wrapped around the front of his throat, he froze grinding against Raul's clenched ass cheeks.

"I didn't tell you to stop, baby boy." His Daddy braced his right hand on Pure's chest, and the left was contracting just enough to restrict his breathing but not cut it off.

His Daddy's head was thrown back, his muscular body arched and rode him. Their sweaty skin slapped together, their voices rang out in the silence, and anyone nearby would know that Daddy was asking his boy to fuck him. He used his bigger bulk to flip them until he was on top, his wider hips forcing his Daddy's to part them wider.

In the dim light coming through the tent, he watched his cock fuck into his Daddy's stretched hole. Raul's hand was still around his throat had fire rushing through his veins, and then his Daddy was jacking his cock to match his pace.

"Make Daddy feel it."

His sac tightened, and he fell forward with his mouth desperately searching for his Daddy's, and then he was filling the latex. An answering wet heat spread between their bellies. His Daddy took his mouth in a brutal kiss.

"Fuck, boy, that dick was made for Daddy's ass."

He kept stroking into his Daddy with shallow thrusts until it was too much and he slipped free. They kissed and touched, both slowly coming down. When their breathing leveled off from harsh pants to deep and even, Raul cleaned them up with a discarded t-shirt.

"Did I do okay, Daddy?" The insecurity that flared in the lessening of post-orgasmic bliss made him ask.

"You were perfect, baby boy. Daddy loved being your first."

Raul stroked his back as his Daddy positioned him with his face buried in Raul's neck. They shared more kisses and whispered words. He opened his mouth to tell Raul, his Daddy, how he felt but forced it back. He was terrified that all the changes would be too much. Tomorrow, when they were both clear-headed and not relaxed from sex, he would confess then.

HELL HAS FOUND THEM

*E*xplosions rang out, smoke and the stench of burned flesh filled his nose, and his eyes burned. He'd lost sight of Pure. His boy was out there in the open. He fell to the ground as Horace called a warning and a round passed so close that he could feel it displace the air over his shoulder where he was tucked down.

"Pure headed east, Freddie had his Six, but that boy was moving fast."

"Find him," he ordered, and Horace disappeared without argument.

He took several deep breaths, jumped to his feet, and took off running in the direction the shots had come from. He didn't have time to think about the one that had hit the ground an inch from Pure. How the hell did they find them? Twigs and leaves crunching beneath his boots were overshadowed by the crackling of the fires where the explosions had sounded.

His heart was beating fast, and sweat dampened the t-shirt he'd dragged on. None of them had time for vests. Whoever was out there was on the move, and they needed to take them out before they got to his team—to Pure. He slowed his steps in the pre-dawn darkness that was only illuminated by the flickering of flames. Kept low. Listening for the even pace of steps. A quickened harsh breath.

A single shot rang out, and the shrill screams of a dying man drowned out everything else. He heard the panicked calls of the bastards sent in after them. He focused, counted individual voices, and heard four. Five by five team. Small but effective. The downed man screamed for help only to be met with men yelling for him to shut up.

He circled, hid in the shadows and tried to pick out shapes. He spotted Freddie alone and tried to ignore his fear when he couldn't see Pure nearby.

He jumped as another shot preceded more screams, two down only three to go. The beam of a flashlight flashed seconds before he saw the muzzle flare. He followed the line of fire, and he started off at a run as the fucker's aim was true. Pure flinched but never stopped. He didn't hesitate to aim and shoot as he squeezed the trigger, controlled bursts, conserving his ammo.

The beam danced in the dimness as it tumbled through the air when the bastard fell. Just as he reached the downed man, Pure was nowhere to be seen. He crouched down, cursing as the tree exploded right next to his head. Flying bark and wood stinging his cheek.

Stay on the move, Raul, your boy needs you alive.

Screams of dying men came from four different directions, which meant there was still one out there.

"You'll never make it out of here alive," an enraged male voice said, and he froze at the sight in front of him when the trees opened to a small clearing.

"I'm a sniper by trade, but for you..." Pure's voice held no emotion. "For you, I want up close and personal."

Pure had the barrel of his forty-five beneath a greasy looking man's chin. From that distance, he could see the overwhelming hatred in the man's eyes.

"He's dead whether I live or die."

"Maybe I'll just keep you alive."

Quickly Pure lowered the weapon and fired once into the man's knee. The stranger tried to lean forward, but Pure's grip in his hair was too tight, then the barrel was right back where it was.

"There's one, now, names, and if I get no names, there's another knee, maybe that sorry excuse for a dick is next."

A snapping of a twig as he entered the clearing made him raise his arm, and he squeezed his trigger, three shots echoed at once. The man fell, the shotgun falling from his hands and then he turned to check on Pure, to find Pure and the man both on the ground. Blood covered Pure's side, and his chest moved as if struggling to take in each breath.

"Pure," he yelled as he knelt beside his boy.

"Did I get him?" Pure wheezed.

"Yeah, baby, you did."

"Ya...gotta go."

"I'm not going anywhere."

Never in the years he'd done this job or worked with Trenton had terror caused him to shake. His boy was bleeding, fighting for each breath. Fear, rage, and helplessness.

"We have a man down, shotgun to the lower left side. Labored breathing." Freddie was speaking somewhere in the distance. Coordinates were relayed.

Horace had his shirt off and pressed to the wound.

"Sin and Saint have the chopper. They're on the move."

He leaned down, Pure's face in his hands and pressed a kiss to his lips. "You gotta hold on for me. Help is coming."

Pure weakly pushed at his chest, rasping as he attempted to order him to go. He wasn't running. That's what got them in this situation.

"Hey, don't close those pretty blues. Tell me something good."

"Not a lot—"

"Tell me," he demanded.

"You would have made pretty, feral babies."

He forced a laugh, and Pure began to cough, blood trickling from the corners of his mouth.

"We still have time."

Just as he was about to yell for an ETA on the chopper, a roar above them signaled help had arrived, and the trees surrounding the clearance started to dance from the spin of the rotors. He covered Pure's body to protect him from debris. He glanced upward in time to see Sin rappelling to the ground with the bright yellow rescue basket, another larger figure just above.

Gibson, the Powers Fire Chief touched down, then Sin and him were in movement to Pure.

"What do we got?"

"Thirty-year-old male, shotgun blast to the lower left side. Possible punctured lung. It was at thirty feet."

"The shot would've dispersed and lost power at that distance. Pure, hey, we're going to check you over and then load you up. They're waiting for you at the hospital. We're going to get you stable and move you to Atlanta."

He held tight to Pure's hand as Gibson worked on him, checking his stats and dressing the wound. Sin was readying the basket to lift Pure out. He wanted to demand answers. Then the monitor signaled an alarm, and the line went flat.

"We don't have time to stabilize in the field...let's move. I have a portable de-fib in the chopper."

Everything was chaos, from the first shot fired no more than an hour ago maybe more, until they rushed to get Pure in the basket.

"Daddy's coming for you, decide now, run or stay and fight," Sin whispered in his ear.

All he could do was stand there helpless as he watched his boy ascend. Would he live or die? He'd waited too long—fucked up too much. Tried to be noble and what did it get him, his boy fighting for his life and he wasn't there to watch over him.

"Come on, man, let's get back to camp, we can still make a run—"

"No, Horace, I've run enough, my boy doesn't make it then I don't really have anything to run for." He tapped his weapon against his thigh as he dragged ass behind Horace and Freddie back to camp. Bullet holes riddled the tents that were turned on their sides. The two men started clearing out the ruined gear and starting a bonfire.

"You know that's evidence, right?"

"What are they gonna do, lock us up?" Freddie started the fire.

He stumbled onto a stump, tossed his weapon aside, and rested his face in his hands. Then he waited for Pelter to arrive. Days of running and worrying, the sense of dread that his boy was already gone, weighed him down. If Pure died, he had nothing left because his career was over. All he would have were bittersweet memories of his boy's first time. The ultimate bliss. How would that hold him over?

His days were numbered. The minute the doors closed behind him was his death sentence. He could fight but for how long, and did he have anything to fight for anymore?

"Raul?"

He turned his head as Pelter's voice came from behind him. The big, dark-skinned man gave him a look that didn't fill him with hope.

"I'm sorry."

He hung his head as he pushed to his feet and put his arms behind his back. The cool steel of handcuffs pinched his wrists and desolation filled him. Never in his life had he allowed himself to be defeated. All he knew was fighting out of a corner and with Pelter's mournful *I'm sorry*, his world collapsed around him.

His rights being read to him were no more than a low drone, and as he was led away from the clearing all he could think was he hadn't told his boy what Pure meant to him. He hadn't made the promises he knew Pure craved. A simple four-letter word, one short sentence, and when he'd had the opportunity, he'd let it go assuming he'd have another day—another time.

Their time had run out, and all he had were regrets.

THE SLAMMING OF JAIL DOORS

*T*welve hours ago, the doors of his cell slammed behind him with a sense of finality. The one person he was allowed to speak with had treated him as if he were a stranger. Peaches' disappointment was clear in her cold professionalism as she told him he was being transferred the next morning had kept him awake all night. Every time he'd asked about his boy, no one had answered him. They walked a wide berth by his cell. He'd ignored the food brought by Heidi.

He closed his eyes countless times only to see the lifeless body of Pure passing like a specter behind his lids. The macabre torture intensified by the unknown. He felt them tormenting him, refusing to acknowledge his need for one shred of good news—a bit of hope. As he paced, his steps echoed in the cavernous space of the basement holding cells of the Sheriff's department.

The transport would be there any minute for him. Was the person wanting to kill him at the end of the transport or behind the walls of state prison? He'd lost count of all the people he'd taken down. As soon as he arrived, the battle for survival began.

Hundreds of inmates holding a grudge. Would he even recognize the danger before it was too late?

"Van's here."

Pelter's voice made him pivot, and he saw the regret on the other man's face. He knew Pelter had helped as much as he could, but he had his own boys and family to think about. He wouldn't thank him on the chance someone listened too closely.

"Pure?"

"No news yet."

"Is there news and you're just not telling me?"

"He got hurt on a job. Once we know something, you'll be the next to know."

A small sense of relief came over him at the knowledge that they'd at least covered his boy's ass. Everyone had their stories to stick to, and since he was going down for life, if he survived to trial, he wasn't going to be allowed in the loop. He needed to get used to no longer being part of the team. Although, Pure's trust was broken, that meant his boy would be moving on as long as they could keep Pure from implicating himself.

All he'd wanted was to make sure his boy was safe. But were they telling him the truth, did Pure make it to the hospital? He couldn't ask further questions on the off-chance that his boy wasn't out of the woods. He rubbed his chest through the stiff material of his orange jumpsuit. They'd confiscated his clothes for forensic testing.

"Horace and Freddie?" They hadn't done anything but agree to shelter them for a few days. He didn't want them punished for a favor. He'd always owe them a debt for putting their lives and freedom on the line out of nothing more than loyalty to Pure. Horace and Freddie had helped keep his boy safe.

"Peaches is dealing with them. The suspects who trespassed on their property were heavily armed and with the amount of evidence, more than likely it'll be a justified shooting. But the D.A is also not happy with the fact that they appeared to destroy evidence in a rather conspicuous bonfire." Pelter's frustration clear as he spoke. "They are being ordered to undergo some psychological testing as Peaches is using severe childhood trauma as a defense and entering their records into evidence. What was done to them hinders their perception of right and wrong."

No one was privy to much about their pasts, but after seeing their bodies, they had lived through hells most couldn't imagine.

"I guess no one is coming to say goodbye."

He understood the abandonment, the distance the Crews were putting between him and them, but he'd never felt loneliness this overpoweringly heavy. He really didn't have anyone left. No crew, no family, and worse, no Pure. That would always be the hardest to accept. He had to be strong though, if— no when his boy survived—he wanted him to move on. He was reluctantly accepting that the moment that the doors had locked behind him, his fate was already sealed.

"Raul, man, I wish there was something I could say or do. Trenton has always gone above and beyond. Made fucked up choices to protect themselves and family, but this...this is an innocent victim and overwhelming evidence that you did it."

"What do they have?"

"Eyewitness accounts of you at the bar, a few even claimed that you were seen leaving with the man." Pelter stuck his arms through the spaces between cold metal to rest on one of the crossbars. The man laced his thick fingers together as if thinking of what to say next and how.

He knew the truth, but sometimes, justice cared nothing about the facts. Justice was making a statement—they didn't care who paid as long as their approval and conviction rates labeled them the best.

"Hair, fiber, and blood evidence that they say shows you were there at the time of the murder. If this is a frame job, I don't know who the fuck you pissed off with these kinda strings to pull."

"I don't have contact with them, but someone needs to tell my mom and dad. I have a feeling this is going to be a public trial. Every bit of dirty information."

"I won't say you're not right. I'll see what I can do."

"Dad's a former cop...he's gonna want to prepare Mom for the backlash."

"Raul, keep your back to the wall and cooperate. You're gonna have no allies inside. And the biggest bitch, we still have no idea who's coming for you. You may have worked with cops, but you won't get any special consideration. You're going to general population. There's going to be no cushy protective custody for you."

He thanked Pelter because the man had given him more information than he should've, but he needed to know how bad it was. When they locked him up, they would come for him from all angles. Cops hated him for the rules he broke. Inmates held grudges, especially for heavy time. Officers would know his rep, gay and brown. He was asking for correction officers to turn his back at the wrong moment.

Two Marshalls entered the holding area, quickly opened his cell and he was outfitted with cuffs and shackles. They were tight enough that his fingers and toes went numb within a minute. The drag of the chain on the cement and the rattle of the cuffs, but no one spared him a glance or helped as he ascended the steps, then was led out the back to the awaiting transport van.

"Can I have a minute with my client?" Peaches stopped them as they were opening the door.

The two Marshalls stepped away.

"When you get inside, find Benito Feeley, he has orders to keep you alive until trial. He owes me one, but if anyone asks, I never said a fucking word. It's just between him and me, none of his Crew know. So keep your head down, don't get yourself stomped and find him."

"Why?" he asked.

"Listen, Raul. I know how things work. I've spent over half my life as a defense attorney. I know when my clients are guilty or not. You're getting jammed up on charges. I'll do my best to get you out, but until then staying alive is all on you. My influence only goes so far. I understand why you ran, but it's not going to help you in the eyes of the jury and the sentencing phase. You should've ran a helluva lot farther when you had the chance."

Peaches stepped back, and the two men secured him in the van. There was a man in a uniform sitting in the back seat, armed, and he knew no escape awaited him. His body tensed as the door slammed and too quickly, they were on their way to Atlanta, then to Texas where he'd stand trial. He had to prepare himself to sit and wait—no bail would be issued. All he had to look forward to was watching his back while he had three hots and a cot provided for him.

Part of him already knew his best-case scenario was getting killed quickly and worst, rotting in a cell until he was old and gray. He'd rather fight for his freedom than give up and lose. Lots of people spent the rest of their lives behind bars, professing their innocence until someone strapped them down and put needles in their arms. He didn't want to throw away his hope. Deep down though, it was just a matter of time before he stood in a courtroom and listened to a judge announce that he'd just be another statistic.

WHEN WOULD THEY ANSWER HIM?

*T*wo weeks passed which had started with his arraignment, denial of bail as he was considered a danger to society and a flight risk. His trial was scheduled for two months out to give his attorney and the District Attorney's office time to gather evidence and wait for testing from state and independent labs. He wasn't surprised, he'd expected it, and they were still trying to find his accomplice.

Peaches' visits were short and brutal, with no mention of the outside world. He used his t-shirt to wipe the sweat from his face as he worked out in the yard. His gaze never stopped scanning his surroundings. He couldn't relax until he was locked in at night, but in those brief hours of respite, his thoughts and dreams tortured him with thoughts of his boy.

They still wouldn't tell him if Pure was okay. The longer the freeze-out went, the more he thought Peaches was attempting to save him from the truth. He'd found Benito and learned that the man was a reluctant ally. Peaches apparently meant blackmail when she said her client owed her a favor.

He walked over the bench where Benito sat, his steel hued hair and scarred face kept everyone at a distance. Benito was serving three consecutive life terms for a series of murders back in the eighties. Peaches had gotten four of seven murder charges dropped due to lack of evidence, and was still working on appeal processes to get him a retrial. Rumors were when the crime boss he worked for needed information, Benito was the best at his job. Some of his victims weren't identified due to the removal of limbs, teeth, and other identifying marks. One of them had died of shock after the man skinned the victim alive.

He didn't like owing the man a debt, but since he'd arrived, he'd escaped numerous attacks with nothing more than a few more scars.

"You gotta piece of ass on the outside?" Benito asked.

"I do, maybe." He sighed and leaned over to rest his forearms on his knees as he looked out at the men littering the workout yard. "Last time I saw him, he was flatlined and being flown away from me. What about you?"

"Naw, man, you get that sentence that says you're an inmate until you die, you suddenly ain't got much to offer."

He wondered if that was going to be him one day. It had already started. Peaches visited in a professional capacity but shared nothing from his life—his former life.

"Inside, you occasionally find a bitch to bend over for ya for a bit of protection."

"Peaches said—"

"Yeah, Peaches, that's one hardened bitch right there. I seen men beg for the chair after one threat from her. Gotta respect a woman like that. Twenty-five years and she still working my case. Ain't gonna do much good. I ain't ever lied about the man I am. I liked it too much. Took pride in my work. Naw, either someone punches my ticket or I—" Benito paused. "I do it myself before someone bigger and badder than me takes over this place. You better get used to the accommodations, Martinez, because even if you're innocent like all the rest of us claim, you're gonna die here." The man motioned around them.

His gut told him the man was right, but he didn't want to admit it out loud though. He tensed as Benito leaned forward to mimic his position.

"You know a Terrance Traven?" Benito asked.

"Low-level goon trying to make his way to the top. Heard he got shivved five years back or so. He skipped town on a weapons charge, and his bondsman wasn't playing around when he discovered he ran."

"Good memory. His old man who went down on a homicide been making some noise. Silvio or some shit like that. Heard his name was Marvin or something but wanted to sound like his balls were bigger than they were."

"What about it?"

"Seems like he's a member of your growing fan club. You might wanna watch your ass."

"Man, I've seen at least thirty people I collected on since I've been here. If I hadn't been faster, that blade woulda done a helluva lot more damage." The makeshift blade had pierced his side, just under the skin, piercing a layer of fat. He'd lost more blood than anything, then they stitched him and sent him on his way.

"What the fuck you doing here, man?"

"I got asked to take a job. My partner was on another assignment, so I went alone. Job went down, and I headed home. Next thing I know, deputies are at my door and taking me into custody on a warrant. Prosecution claims they have witnesses that said the bartender went back to my room. They got evidence that's pretty tight."

"Who the fuck you piss off with that much clout?"

"The list is long." He felt his lips tug into a smile at the rough chuckle from the other man.

"Don't I know it. See that kid over there?"

He followed as Benito pointed to a scruffy kid, shaking like he was coming down, and talking to a group of guys that looked to be about the same age.

"Yeah, what about him?"

"That's Squeak, violent motherfucker, crazy white boy, but you might wanna make friends. Ain't nothing that boy can't learn. Somehow got himself assigned to the library. One of the C.O.s kinda gotta a hard-on for him. Might be worth using his spectacular blowjob skills."

"Not interested."

"I'd be too afraid his detoxing ass be biting it off, but he'll do anything for a price. You find out his weakness…he might just find you some answers."

Benito didn't say anything else as he pushed to his feet and headed across the yard. As he got up and followed, he pulled his t-shirt over his head and thought about what the man said. He couldn't sit there and wait for good news that wasn't coming. He needed to make a list.

Men who lived the life, they expected their untimely deaths. They signed up for it. He mentally brought up all the names Pure mentioned during those weeks of research.

At the thought of his boy, the loss washed over him again. Dead or alive, he needed to know. Would his boy be waiting for him on the outside or would he be visiting a grave to say his goodbyes? To confess the love he hadn't had the balls or smarts to do before the first battle began.

How long before his memory faded? Pure nothing more than a ghostly outline of disappearing features. He wouldn't remember the softness of his boy's lips or the sound of his laughter. Fantasies of the weight of Pure's head on his chest, the rush of his warm breath, and the softness in his boy's beautiful blue eyes. All of that faded in time, nothing lasts forever, and the years elapsing to erase what used to be tangible items.

He owed it to his boy to get out somehow. His boy had fought so hard for him, possibly made the ultimate sacrifice. Even if he figured out his way to freedom, Pure was it. The one he'd waited for—the one who made him start to believe that dreams weren't childish imaginings. His boy would never get his happily ever after or the future children that had his boy smile.

He'd ruined that, but he had to make amends. Had to make sure that Jenn's sacrifice—her faith in his innocence—was worth it. Reaching out to her terrified him. An apology wouldn't ever be good enough. Pure was all she'd had, and he'd taken that from her.

All he had to do was find a way, he would, but first, he had to survive. To find the person hellbent on enacting justice hands-on; who had enough hatred for him to orchestrate his downfall? People had all kinds of reasons to do the things they did.

Revenge was the biggest. Retribution for a supposed wrong. Yet, everyone was different. People felt justified to do atrocities to people. An abusive husband who thought murdering their spouse for leaving them was acceptable. A shorted baggie in a drug buy. Hell, being looked at in a way that someone found disrespectful. What would cause this level of rage? It had to be more than a bounty. This was personal, and if he didn't find some clues soon, he was going to lose everything, Having his boy taken from him was cruel punishment enough.

He'd always knew that possessing Nicolas would be like attaining the beauty of the sun. Light and warm, comforting after the darkness. His touch had destroyed his boy. His selfishness had put his boy in danger, and now he had to atone for those sins.

PURE AWAKENED WITH NOTHING

*T*hey assured him he'd awakened several times over the past three weeks, but it wasn't until that morning that he'd been coherent enough to take in his surroundings. He wore a brace and was unable to move. The doctors explained that several pellets had shattered a rib that had, in turn, punctured his lung. The subsequent blood loss and trauma, along with a minor infection, had taken him out for the count. He'd heal, this wasn't his first time getting shot and it wasn't his worst.

What was pissing him off was that no one was answering his questions. He remembered the fear in Raul's eyes, and that was it until he'd regained consciousness. His first demand was to see Raul. To know he was okay, but he knew no one else had fought for him. Horace and Freddie would've watched Raul's back. He sensed that Raul had turned himself in once he'd gotten hurt.

He didn't want guilt or despair. His Daddy needed to fight.

He'd barred everyone from his room, no Trenton guys or Crew were allowed. Security had asked Peaches to leave. Looking at them enraged him. He'd never forgive them for the disloyalty they showed. If everyone thought he was overreacting or being unreasonable, he'd stepped outside the law plenty in defense of the Crews. Most of them had bodies hidden—deaths to answer for—and he was no different. Their hypocrisy was more than he could take. He'd taken lives in defense of his teammates without a second thought.

Trust was a huge thing for him. He'd spent too many years covering his ass and not letting anyone close. The Crews were the family he'd always wanted. A life where he never worried about who was at his Six.

"What did I tell you about showing up in my ER?"

His mother's disapproving tone made him smile, and he looked up at her leaning onto the bed. Her perfect arched brows reaching for her hairline.

"No better ER to end up in."

"True enough."

"What's the verdict?"

"Your ribs will take time to heal, and the tear to your lung was a simple enough repair. Another ten feet closer and I would've been picking out a suit for you to be buried in."

Death was something they'd talked about a lot over the years. His time in the military and Trenton, how easily things could go wrong. Her job as a nurse. They both knew tomorrow wasn't a guarantee.

"How much did you cry?"

She rolled her eyes and rubbed his cheek. "Plenty and then I went to the shooting range."

"Best therapy ever. Where's Raul?"

"Texas. He was taken there the day after you were rushed to Atlanta. You were transported by Sin and Saint, with Gibson acting as medic straight from Horace and Freddie's. They didn't have time to stabilize you in Powers."

"When are the cops coming for me?"

"Pelter, Gibson, Sin, and Saint, along with Trenton, came up with you were off on a job and injured in the process."

"I don't forgive them."

"And I understand, but maybe they thought it through. Why was Raul not as a part of the team as the rest? He's been around several years, but he's still the new guy. It's only been a few years where you two have been an exclusive team. How well do we know anyone, Nicolas?"

"I trust him with my life."

"And that is the reason I didn't hesitate to help, but now we have to stay inside the lines on this one. We have to play nice with the men with badges."

"Do I gotta?"

"Unfortunately, yes. You know I see shit in the ER, trauma, and we see the worst of humanity and what people do to it, especially people we're supposed to trust. Now, if you're still free of infection by the end of the week and getting around, I packed us bags. You can't fly until your lung is completely repaired. So, we're heading to Texas to be close to Raul for his incarceration and trial. They denied bail."

"I knew that would happen. I didn't tell him I loved him." As he confessed, tears slipped from the corners of his eyes.

"I'm sure he knows even without the words. You two, I may not like the profession or what he does, but I knew from the way you looked as you talked about him. That smile I always hoped you'd get when you allowed yourself to trust someone."

"I told him he'd make pretty, feral babies."

She snorted and dropped a kiss on his forehead.

"Of course you did. Men love to know their acceptable breeding partners."

"He didn't...he didn't make me feel bad about the things I wanted—want. Raul didn't push...he respected my limits. He didn't make me feel dirty."

"There is nothing dirty about you. The bastard who created that hatred inside of you...the sense of degradation...he's the one who should've suffered. But your emotions and thoughts were violated along with your body. Strength is being able to—"

"Love past the pain." He finished the single line that she'd spoken to him the night it happened. The words he'd inked into his skin the day he'd returned to Powers with the determination to find a way through.

"Love isn't a cure-all, baby, it's just what helps us move beyond that which attempted to destroy us. You were my strength the day you were born. Your first cries were what eased the betrayal. My gift for surviving. And you need to do the same for Raul, be his gift.

"And maybe search for a bit of forgiveness. At least for Gage because I tell you, that man is free with the spanking threats. And that is one sexy man. I might just misbehave to give him an excuse."

"He's got a boyfriend."

He appreciated her change of topic, and her attempt to lighten the mood. He had so much he had to do, plans to make, and he wasn't quite ready to start mending fences. The resentment was still too strong.

"I'm aware but I ain't blind."

"You need to start dating."

"There is this very handsome new ER doctor, considerably younger but, let's just say I'd totally ignore that if he even hinted, but he's been off the schedule. So, maybe he was temporary."

We laughed and hugged, but there was still an elephant in the room. The fact that a few feet closer and he wouldn't be there, but they put that fear and pain into the embrace. Celebrating silently that they were both alive.

"Mr. Warner, Nurse Warner." A deep voice with a hint of an accent made us part.

"Dr. Fenway, are you slumming? I noticed you were off the board."

He rolled his lips between his teeth at her thickening southern accent as he studied the man in the doorway. Slim and elegant with that silver at the temples thing that made men a bit sexier. When his mother developed a crush, she went all out.

"Very much so, I was asked to do a week rotation. May I examine you, Mr. Warner?"

"Nicolas is fine or Pure. It's my nickname at work. Not many people other than Mom call me Nicolas anymore."

The doctor spoke as he checked his surgical incision, tested for tenderness, and the entire time, Pure watched his mom staring at the doctor. He smiled at her blush when she noticed him studying her. He loved that she was coming more out of her shell every year. It began with nursing school and her job in the emergency room. She'd found her place and as weird as he'd found it, he wanted his mom to find someone.

"Nurse Warner, your son is healing perfectly. Nicolas, because of the infection, we want to make sure you don't relapse so we'll be keeping you a few more days."

"Her name is Jenn," he said.

"Jenn, it's a very beautiful name. I'm still new, and my former employer was stricter about doctor/staff formality. Well, we're going to lower your pain medication to wean you off. I'll see you tomorrow morning for rounds, and maybe we can determine a definite time to prepare you for discharge."

"I'll be taking personal leave to stay with him while he heals."

"Very good. Nurse...Jenn, Nicolas, I'll leave you to visit."

The doctor left, and Mom watched him the entire way. "Shame about the doctor's coat."

"He has the cutest, roundest ass I've ever seen. I get nothing done when he works."

He laughed and groaned. "Don't make me laugh."

"Get well," she said as she sat on the side of his bed. "Everything is ready to go when they discharge you. We'll do everything within our power to get Raul home."

"I know, but what if he doesn't—"

"He'll survive. He knows he has you to come home to."

He hoped that was enough. They'd spoken about the possibility that he wouldn't be found not guilty. He was told to move on, but how could he? He'd waited years to find that one person who would make the darkness fade. Three weeks he'd laid in a hospital bed, what if no one was giving his Daddy updates? What if Raul thought he was dead? He had to get out of there, but he needed to be patient. He had to make it back to the top of his game or what use was he?

HIS BOY CAME FOR HIM

*H*e dropped his book to his chest as a baton banged against the bars of his cell. He marked his page and rolled from the lower bunk.

"Martinez, you have a visitor."

"Who is it?" He was hoping Peaches was coming back with more information. The weeks were passing too quickly but slowly also. He still wasn't given information about Pure or the case. Squeak apparently wasn't as skilled at cock sucking as he was informed because he still hadn't gotten the files for the names he'd asked for. The kid wasn't as burnt as he'd first thought, but that wasn't saying much.

"How the fuck should I know?"

The officer called for the cell to open, and he stepped out. He tried to push down his rage as he was shackled and handcuffed. He had one man in front and another behind him as he was escorted through the prison. At one point, he caught Benito's gaze as he passed his cell. He shrugged at the lifting of the man's brow.

His curiosity and suspicion grew as he was led in the opposite direction of the meeting rooms for prisoners and their attorneys.

That meant it wasn't an official visit. Which meant he had no idea who would be on the other side of the glass. A buzzer sounded, and he was led down the narrow space with bolted down stools and cubicles. There was a community visiting area for prisoners with privileges.

He froze as he caught sight of his visitor. His boy looked thinner and paler. He lowered himself onto the stool and loathed the glass that separated them. He couldn't stop staring and fumbled the receiver. It took him two tries before he pressed it to his ear. He'd started to give up. Accepted that he was alone.

"Hey, baby boy."

"Hi, are you okay?"

"Yeah, ready to go home." He leaned forward, and his boy did the same.

"I'm working on it. I rented a furnished apartment here. Mom's staying to help me get settled then she has to get home to this hot younger doctor."

"Hot, huh?"

"The whole sexy British thing doesn't really do it for me."

"It better not, you know who owns you, whether I'm in here or not."

"What a possessive Daddy."

"You're asking for punishment."

"Yeah, yeah, you were a lot more reckless before you got in my pants."

He wanted to kiss his boy's curved lips and savor that Pure was alive. Still there to joke like they used to post jobs.

"What was the damage?" he asked as he saw his boy shifted uncomfortably. He wanted to be able to touch and kiss, check every inch of his boy to make sure he was okay.

"Shattered rib, but I'm fine. Nothing that won't heal."

"I hate this fucking glass. No one told me shit about you. As far as I knew you could've been dead and I just want to check you over."

"One day soon. Now, what can you tell me?"

"There's my Pure." He knew him so well, and he could see the wheels already turning. "I got a few names that might be good for some information, but so far it hasn't panned out."

"I got it covered. Whatever you need, just give me a list. I brought all my supplies with me."

"You know how sexy you are when I think about you in your tactical gear."

"I do."

"Brat."

"You can take care of that when you come home."

"I'm keeping track."

Raul snorted, and he couldn't help smiling at his boy. Alive but maybe not safe. "You go nowhere without a vest."

"It's in the car with Mom, and she has her own."

"Send her home."

"Mom said you'd say that and she told me to tell you...no. She's armed, and she's a better shot than you."

"Ouch, baby boy, way to hurt my feelings."

"I taught Mama everything she knows. Alone in the city, her job can get dangerous, and I got her a concealed permit."

"I should have a harder time picturing your flowery apron-wearing mama carrying, but it's pretty easy after meeting her."

"Well, all I'm saying is she can take care of herself, and she's only here for a few weeks to take care of my bandages, then she's headed out. She's going to run interference for me from back home."

"I should tell you to cut your losses and go on with your life."

"But you're not, because I need you home and safe. And you need me here. I'll do what needs to be done in the streets while you work everything from your side. Who do I need to contact?"

"I have a truce with Benito Feeley. He's watching my back for now."

"Find out what'll keep him loyal for the time being. I left you a little something. I'm sure they're searching every inch of the package at the moment. I got a landline for collect calls and a P.O. Box. We gotta go a bit old school."

"Nothing wrong with old school."

They spoke until the officer behind him said it was time to go.

"Baby boy—"

"Tell me when you're out of here."

"What if—"

"There's no what if. You'll be out, and if not, not a bad city. I have plenty of skills to find another job. Weekly visits are better than nothing."

"Nicolas."

"Ouch, going stern Daddy on me. You tell me what you need, and you'll get it."

"Will do."

"Time to go, Martinez."

He reluctantly hung up the receiver, and he noticed his boy's hands fist as the officer jerked him up from the stool. He also didn't miss the way his boy seemed to memorize the bastard for Pure's crosshairs. Outwardly his baby boy was calm, but after years of careful study—anticipating his boy's moods—Pure had reached homicidal.

I'll be fine, he mouthed, and Pure nodded, but he knew his agreement wouldn't last if Pure could get his hands on the C.O.

He was pushed forward but caught one more look at his beautiful boy's face. Pure was alive and close by, that would have to be enough. When they made it back to his cell, he was released from his restraints and locked back up. He picked up the box with the ripped paper that sat on the small desk. There was a letter with a number and address on the envelope—supplies for him to write.

"Now, baby boy, you have outdone yourself," he whispered to himself as he lifted out the book. A page was marked with a poem card. It was a mix of regular and block letters, an alphanumeric code. Block letters were numbers. It was the way his boy had written passwords and account numbers. They'd shared that information in case of emergencies. It wasn't something people would pay attention to, but his boy knew he'd notice.

He sat down to get to work until it was time to line up for lunch. That night he'd work on a letter with the information his boy needed to handle an outside investigation. He needed someone he could trust to do what was necessary, and his boy was close enough to see.

"Visitor?"

He jerked his gaze up to find Benito staring through the bars.

"Yeah."

"Squeak has something for you. You might want to take a trip to the library after lunch."

"From the look on your face, I'm not gonna like it."

"Man, the names he has for you, you're gonna need someone who's willing to go above and beyond."

"No one more vicious than my boy when he needs to be."

"I still got a few friends on the outside if your boy needs some backup."

"Why?"

"I got shit to atone for, and against my better judgment, I don't want to kill you."

"Thanks, I think."

"Remember, after lunch."

"Got it."

He waited for the man to leave and looked down at the partial message he'd deciphered.

I love you. If you don't survive, I'll show up at your funeral just to shoot your casket.

His boy had a way with words. He tucked the plastic-coated card back into the book along with the piece of paper. They'd call lunch soon. He'd have names to send Pure.

He didn't want to get his hopes up too much, but things

appeared to be coming together. He knew he had time on him for the escape, but that was better than a life sentence on top of that. He stood and paced the length of his cell, five steps to the wall and as many back to the bars. The last time he was in a space this small, Little had locked him in the weapons cage. Little had thought they needed sex lessons with the puppets he'd picked up. His boy had looked sexy when he'd taken that shot at Little. He smiled to himself, his boy was alive, and that's all that mattered. His freedom was second. Pure's happiness would always come first, and what would make his boy happy was them together. He'd do everything in his power to get out of there, except putting his boy's life on the line.

He needed to make sure his boy had backup, and he knew the Trenton guys were out as an option. That meant he was going to make a deal with a sadistic psychopath. What could possibly go wrong?

ENEMIES WERE CLOSER THAN THEY EXPECTED

*H*e'd received a letter a day for five days and had them laid out—each one was deciphered, and he was shuffling through files to get rid of as much of his electronic footprint as possible. What he was done with was burned in the fireplace in his temporary apartment. As fast as the list grew, the more he marked off when he found they were dead or supposedly living the good life.

"Talk it out."

He turned to find his mom standing in the entryway of the kitchen with her suitcase beside her feet. As much as she wanted to stay, she was called back to work because all hell had broken loose without her.

"I just have this bad feeling that…they're out there and closer than I'm comfortable with."

"Raul said you were going to meet some people that could help you."

"Yeah, but I trust him, but I'm just not so sure about taking reinforcements from a hitman."

"At least you'll be cautious."

"Yeah." He went through some more papers. "There's this guy

inside named Squeak. He trades sexual favors for information he's paid to find. The kid's record reads like a manual on how to build the perfect serial killer. He was serving time in Juvie before he fucking hit puberty."

"But has his information panned out?"

"A bit but not fast enough."

"You have a month and a half until the trial."

"I don't know if Raul has that kinda time."

"He will. He's not going to leave you alone."

"I don't want him worrying about me, Mom. He needs to worry about his own ass."

She scoffed, and he accepted her hug when she wrapped her arms around his waist. "Not going to happen. You mean everything to him. And you two will do whatever is necessary to get back to each other. You have to accept that he's at least going to be doing time for the escape."

"The one I planned and executed without his knowledge."

"There is that. What about the victim?"

"Good kid, no boyfriends, no record." He picked up the file on the victim. "Working his way through college as a bartender. His boss and co-workers said he wasn't the type to leave the bar with a customer. You don't buy your meat where you make your bread."

"A lovely analogy."

"Good advice, though."

"Advice you didn't keep. Maybe you should hit that bar, see if maybe someone noticed someone who may have paid more attention than the others. I'm sure they flashed a picture of Raul when they went to the bar."

He knew she was right. He hated to admit that people noticed when a rough, biker-looking brown man was hitting on a pretty white boy bartender. The area where the motel and truck stop bar were located wasn't in the best part of the county. It was positioned right off the highway. No one would notice a stranger as truckers and travelers were in and out every day. Familiar faces such as Raul's would be remembered, and they hadn't used a picture lineup. The investigators took a single photo and then had them come in to look at a lineup in person. Raul would've stuck out.

"They showed a single picture."

"Well, that was amateur behavior. Why didn't Peaches try to get the lineup thrown out?"

He tossed the file aside. A friend had somehow worked out a way to get him a copy of everything they had so far on the investigation. "I guess she had her reasons."

"Baby, you need friends, call someone, at least Gage, maybe Little."

"I can do this on my own."

"I won't bitch about it anymore, just promise to think about it."

"I will, I promise."

"That's all I can ask."

"You want me to drive you to the airport?" She was leaving her car so he'd have a vehicle to get around in and they hoped if the plates were run, her name wouldn't cause any immediate red flags.

"No, I have a car coming to take me. As soon as I land, I'll call you. Remember, the safety deposit box has your new IDs and passports, along with your prepaid phones and cards. I pulled some more cash. There's also a rental in your alias at long-term parking."

They'd rented the vehicle and used a magnetic hide-a-key. He appreciated everything she was doing, but she was dishing out a lot of the operation's expenses.

"Mom, that's your savings."

"How many years have you taken care of me? How many times did you pay for my books or school? I know you can afford it, but me shifting around some money won't make any waves.

You, son, are the one who's going to be making a lot of people nervous. I want you to have your escape plan. Not that you're going to need it."

"Nice save."

"Nicolas, you know I'm going to worry, it's what I do. Unless there's an emergency, I'll see you when the trial starts. I already put in the time off at least for the beginning of it. Gotta use all that vacation and personal time."

He hugged her tight but didn't want to let her go. But her phone chiming to let her know her car arrived forced him to release her. He kissed her cheek and gave her a small smile when she placed her hand around his right side where his tattoo was hidden.

"Remember the words, son. And if the worst happens, they need nurses everywhere. Raul will never be alone."

To keep himself from reaching for her, he crossed his arms as she backed away. He was tired and frustrated—his body felt like it weighed a ton. His ribs ached constantly. He hadn't had a full night's sleep in over a month that wasn't induced by painkillers.

He removed his t-shirt and slipped on his vest, securing the straps as he cursed the twinges in his side. His hand hesitated over the bail enforcement badge. He took a deep breath and slipped the chain around his neck. Covering it with his t-shirt. He checked his weapon and slipped it back into the holster, then he clipped it at his waist. He needed to get out, clear his head, and maybe get his brain to start working.

On his way out the door, he grabbed his keys, phone, and hoodie. He set the pressure sensor under the welcome mat and tested it to make sure it alerted his phone. A tiny camera would send footage of anyone who came to his door while he was out. He slowly made his way to the lobby and out onto the busy neighborhood street.

He snorted as he clocked the undercover tailing him before he made it to the steps of the next building. He scanned the area, paused when he reached a shop, and made a show of looking through the front windows. There were at least three people following him

A car screeched to a halt at the curb, and he removed his weapon while flipping the safety. Screams sounded around him, and people began to scatter.

A big guy in an expensive suit and sunglasses that cost a pretty penny stood from the front seat. "Warner, Benito sent us and your man said he was still keeping track."

The back door popped open.

"Or do you want to meet your new friends?"

He slipped into the backseat and held his forty-five Glock and his trigger finger at the ready.

"Nero," the guy introduced himself, "Catch, and that's Moe. Benito said we were to show you the utmost respect and hospitality while you vacation in our cesspool of a city."

"I'm sure that would bring the tourist running. Why are you so interested in helping?"

"We ain't. We owe a debt, and he called in a marker," Nero explained while the other two men remained silent.

They kept checking rearview mirrors and glancing out the back window.

"And I'll admit to a certain…curiosity. Benito would rather kill someone than breathe the same air."

"I know a few people like that."

He took mental notes of streets, how many turns they made, and all at a normal rate of speed. No traffic laws to get them pulled over, except for the occasional wrong turn signal, then they cut hard to head in the opposite direction.

"This is for you." Nero handed him a large brown envelope.

He holstered his weapon and quickly removed the contents. The names on the list were familiar, a list of the who's who of America's Most Wanted Crime Bosses. "And what am I looking at?"

"Your man is good, but your line of work doesn't, well, it ain't making y'all friends. These are the heads of families that have ended up in prison or had a close relative earn a life or death sentence. There's one on there that you should pay close attention to, Marilee Corza. The most vicious Mafia Princess to ever run her own Crew. Her old man sent her to England about ten years ago when he got hit with racketeering and murder charges."

"This name wasn't in my files."

"It wouldn't be…neither of them had a price on their heads. Martinez grabbed a witness that ran. Brought him back to testify, all secretive and shit. The operation he freelanced for back then had a deal that he'd take care of off-the-books assignments and the D.A. and cops would look the other way on occasion. The guy he brought back snitched and got a clean break, probably lazy in suburbia somewhere."

"A decade is a long time to hold a grudge."

"True. But let's just say that there's been some shit going around that some serious money changed hands and there's rumors of a new trial. Seems Daddy's Princess wasn't Corza's kid. His old lady cheated. Seems Corza got rid of the wife and brought his underage *step*daughter into the bedroom to replace the cheating bitch. There ain't nothing she wouldn't do for him, and he sent her out of the country to keep her safe. Corza would do anything for that girl. A month ago, she took up residence in the family home, and she's rebuilding the empire.

"Can't say for sure, but a few people have whispered that she slit her nanny's throat for looking at Corza a second too long. She was twelve. Imagine that ten years later, and the princess is looking to become queen."

He thumbed through the photos of a girl with a sweet face, but that level of physical and emotional abuse and conditioning could warp anyone.

"Raul just brought a witness back. He didn't take the stand."

"Don't make no difference. They want him gone. Corza is due to be returned to prison here in preparation for motions for his retrial. He can't take the chance the witness spilled to the bounty hunter."

"Where Raul is awaiting trial?"

"Yep." Nero glanced back at him. "Loyalty is an amazing thing, man, but in this case, she's about to rain down hell on these streets. She's determined to get her daddy out and then take over the entire city just like in the good old days."

No fucking wonder they hadn't found anything. Raul probably didn't do more than take the assignment, complete it, and move on to the next. They never worried much about what happened after their jobs finished. Beyond the payday, their involvement ended after they signed the paperwork. If all of this were true, he needed an army, and that was something he didn't have.

He needed a plan and a lot more firepower. In order to succeed, he needed to remove the head of the snake or at least the one walking the street. The woman needed to be taken out. That also meant he was going to need to thin her crew a bit.

"You have someone who could help me out with some equipment?"

"As long as you got the money to spend, I can find you whatever you need."

"Let's find a place for dinner, and I'll make you a list."

THEY COULDN'T HIDE FOREVER

"*Ya* gotta be fucking kidding me?" He tried not to destroy the letter in his hands, but the paper crinkled where it was clutched in his fists. His boy had just hung up on him in the middle of Raul telling him to get his ass back to Powers.

This was not what he needed, and the call he'd made to his boy had met with stubbornness. He punched in Trenton's office number and Gage's extension. He waited impatiently for the man to answer.

"Gage." The man growled into the phone.

An inconvenienced Gage wasn't the man to ask for help, but he was out of options. Especially when his boy was going to start a one-man war, and there wasn't anything he could do to stop him. Not when he was locked up with no allies to call.

"Don't hang up."

"Not in much of a position to be giving orders."

He rubbed his hand over his face and tugged at his longer goatee. "Don't start."

"What the fuck do you want? Since your boy up and quit,

pulling a complete disappearing act, and you, well, we know where you are."

"Pure's about to make an exit."

"I'm listening."

"I did a job about a decade ago. As far as I knew it was just your usual grab a runner, bring him back for a nice payday. Seems I dragged a witness back to testify against a crime boss. Name's Corza."

"And?"

"You're not helping me here."

"Give me a reason."

"You need to find my boy and make sure he doesn't"—he sighed—"I'm gonna lose him, Gage."

"Where's he staying?"

"Don't know. He uses a P.O. Box, but I got a landline number. All I know is he's in the city."

"Give it to me."

He recited the number. "Pure's out in the cold. I got him a few people to watch his back, but he's gonna go solo on this job."

"He's smarter than that."

"My boy is too enraged. He's out for blood."

"You should control your boy better. I would've suggested some extra correction and less letting him get shot."

"Quit being a dick and help me. I can do my time or die, doesn't matter to me as long as my boy is still breathing."

"I'll see what I can do. I'm sure Pure's running everything under an alias."

"I know Jenn was staying, but I think she had to get back to work."

"I'm due for a visit. She's been asking for a spanking for two months."

"She's packing, man."

"And she's lethal, but I know her weakness. Just cover your ass."

"I'm trying. Thanks, man."

"Don't thank me. This is for Pure. He was sane until you gave him the dick."

"I missed you, Gage."

He pulled the receiver away from his ear as Gage hung up on him. He was feeling the love today. He folded the note and exited the room where the phones were kept. He hurried to find Benito and get info about the men watching his boy. He jogged to Benito's cell and stopped outside.

"Who's watching him?"

The man stood up from his seat on the bunk and came to lean on the wall next to the opened cell door.

"My cousin, Nero, and a couple of his friends."

"Name Corza mean anything to you?"

"Wow, when you fuck up, you go all out. No wonder these motherfuckers been preparing like they 'bout to meet God."

He rolled his shoulders as he tried to ignore the way the pressure built behind his eyes as his blood pressure started to skyrocket.

"I know what info my boy sent me, but what about his daughter?"

"I don't know what you want me to tell ya, rumors of a hitlist been making the rounds, but it's all speculation. Corza and his daughter cross some pretty fucked up lines. Their partnership is what Hell looks like. If you fucked over Corza, I hope you made your peace and said goodbye to that pretty boy of yours."

"You're not fucking helping—"

Benito raised his hand to cut him off, and he clenched his teeth and tried to keep his fists from clenching.

"Nero's been mentioning that she's back in the city and is making plans to have the organization rebuilt and stronger than before Corza got locked down. My former employer has been very interested in the developments. With Corza gone, it left room for lower-level bosses to quickly climb the hierarchy."

The man glanced left, then right to check to make sure they didn't have an audience. The man hadn't shown an ounce of worry in the weeks he'd known him. He remained silent and waited for the man to find his words. If he was going to be of some help, he needed to know what his boy was walking into out there.

"Corza's been in solitary for most of his sentence to keep him from making any calls and only allowed visits from his lawyers. Those who don't fear he'll slit their throats want to be on his good side when he makes it back into the world. Now, loyalty only goes so far...power and money have a way of changing priorities."

"So, his loving daughter is working to get him out to take over?"

"Wouldn't put it past her. Corza trusts no one but her. What's the best way to take down an organization?"

"From the inside. You break down the trust inside, and everyone looks at each other as an enemy. Until they destroy each other while the guilty one just stands back and waits."

"Men can get stupid when they're addicted to their piece. Corza is obsessed with that girl, always was, even before he knew he didn't share DNA."

"Where can we find her?"

"She'll be easy to find. There's a townhouse on S. Vernon, or there's an estate outside the city. A nice quiet place where all the bodies get buried."

He needed to make another call, but there wouldn't be anyone picking up on the other end. He knew his boy, and Pure was already in the field doing recon and mission planning. His boy would have schematics and blueprints, intel on the players. He'd have everything plotted out down to the weather, mostly wind speed and direction.

Curses slipped past his lips at his uselessness. His boy shouldn't be out there alone. He was the only one who should be at his boy's side. One fucking job, one stupid bounty, and a decade later, his boy was paying for his mistake. If not for Benito, he wouldn't even have a name because all he remembered about jobs was if his check cleared.

"Keep your head, man. You ain't gonna do anyone any good. If Corza is headed here, then he planned this down to the smallest fucking detail. He's the type of man to handle his own business… it sets an example. Shows his people that he's not afraid to get his hands dirty. When he comes, you're gonna take the King's crown. Your boy got it handled in the street. Destroy them both."

"What's in it for you?"

"The occasional favor. Nothing more. And to be honest, I'll owe ya for taking Corza out for me. You're the only one who's gonna be able to get close."

"Fair enough."

He narrowed his eyes as Benito's lips curved into a smile that made his skin crawl. Whatever was about to come out of the man's mouth was about to terrify him or piss him off.

"Nero said he took your boy shopping, and from what I hear your boy with a sniper rifle got my straight cousin's interest. Maybe I can meet this boy of yours one day."

"Not in this lifetime, Benito."

"Shame. Always had a thing for vicious boys and girls when I was on the outside."

"Well, my boy is all mine."

"Can't blame a fucker for trying."

"If I make it out, I'll work with Peaches to see about getting you out."

"Appreciate the thought, man, but I gave up that hope a long time ago. Go get some rest or whatever…you're about to go to war."

He nodded and straightened, heading back to his own cell. He stepped inside and rolled onto the bottom bunk. The upper bunk had been empty since he'd arrived and he wondered if someone was watching his back—if Benito had pulled some strings to get him locked up solo.

His brain started analyzing every detail. And it brought back nights of the conference room at Trenton with him and his boy planning their jobs down to the minute detail. Or evenings with take-out on rooftops scouting the perfect sniper post. His boy was handsome and sweet, intelligent and loyal. Years he'd kept his distance out of some sense of decency. He'd wanted his boy to find that dream—the one he'd waited to show up.

He had regret for the time wasted, but Benito was right. They'd separated them, tried to break the team up in an attempt to make them weaker. Only he was more determined to take care of Corza, and he looked forward to telling Corza his empire had fallen.

Gage would take his boy's Six for him. Gage and the team Benito sent would make sure his boy had backup. He'd feel better with the whole Trenton Crew, but that wasn't going to happen. Once Pure's trust was broken, he couldn't forget. He trusted Gage, enough to talk about private matters. Hopefully, that got Gage inside because he wouldn't relax until he got word his boy was safe. They couldn't hide forever. Eventually, their enemies would have to come up for air.

TRENTON TOOK NO PRISONERS

*H*e stared through his scope at the street below, cataloging hardware and picking out the guards trying to act natural. Their cheap suits didn't conceal the bulge of weapons, most likely automatic rifles. There was a guy seated on the stoop about four doors down with the worst damn Hawaiian shirt. His hair greased and swept backward to expose a receding hairline. He counted at least ten men guarding the front. He opened his tablet and checked the cameras he'd placed in the alleyway behind the townhouses.

They weren't hiding in the rear. He counted another six. Not a huge force. An elegant woman had entered with just two men flanking her. One last thing to check, he scanned the building with infrared looking for heat signatures. He wrote down some more notes, to add her and another six people to the list. Small army but it wasn't impossible to take them out.

He'd have to change tactics. He'd probably be able to take out most of the ones out front, but unfortunately, they'd determine his position before the bodies finished hitting the ground. He'd tried every rooftop and attic space, but the angles were all wrong. There were too many opportunities for innocent casualties.

Best option was a soft entry, suppressor or blade. That was a team operation, and he was working with a barely healed rib. His maneuverability was limited. He returned his rifle to the soft case and packed the rest of his equipment into his backpack. He left the transmitter in place to keep up surveillance from his apartment. Nero was arriving later that night.

A team of four wasn't ideal, but it was better than going in solo. He went down the fire escape at the rear and jogged to his car parked at the end of the alley. The ride across the city was filled with more plans and worries, thoughts of Raul and would he be safe. He called an old contact two weeks before, and he was informed the prison transport was due to arrive at any time. They'd told him they'd move Corza with no fanfare.

He'd avoided visiting Raul. They still exchanged coded messages, but the tone of them had turned frosty. That didn't mean Nero wasn't making regular contact with Benito. He made sure Raul had received regular updates. He pulled into a parking spot down the block from his building. He grabbed his case and backpack, then checked his surroundings before exiting.

He kept his head down, avoiding the cameras in case Hunter was running facial recognition all over the city. He wouldn't put it past the hacker. He jogged up to his floor but froze as he noticed the black string on the light-colored welcome mat. He set his things down and removed his weapon. He hugged the wall and approached his door. He forced himself to calm, slowed his breathing, and he peeked through the crack in the door. Nothing was ransacked, the interior looked just as he'd left it.

He pushed the door all the way open, entering, and clearing his blind spots. When his back was pressed to the wall, he pivoted his body as a hand appeared, and tried to strip his gun from his hands. He feigned backward, grabbed a vase in his right hand, and swung, the ceramic exploded. He moved around the corner, raised his weapon, took a deep breath, and started to squeeze, then he froze.

"Fuck, Pure, nice way to greet a guest."

"What the fuck are you doing here, Gage?" He holstered his Glock and retrieved his things from the hallway. When he came back, he slammed the door. He headed for the kitchen without giving Gage a second look.

"Seems you've been misbehaving."

"You're not my Daddy, Gage."

"If I was, you'd be locked up and nursing a very raw ass right now. What the fuck are you doing?"

"I'm handling what I need to," he answered as he started the pot of coffee he'd readied earlier that day.

"You don't take on an OP of this scale alone."

"I have backup."

"It's not us," Gage yelled.

"I'm no longer a part of the *us*, so go home, Gage."

"We didn't betray you, Nicolas."

"Do you know how many kill shots I've taken in defense of y'all? How many bodies I've buried when we knew the target wouldn't stop? And the minute I needed y'all to back me, y'all forget."

"Yes, we dropped the fucking ball. We should've done better. You and Raul should be on a beach in a non-extradition country right now, but that's not what's going down. The only option we have is to erase the threat.

"Corza is arriving at the state prison in forty-eight hours. Peaches has arranged a welcoming party. But first, we have to take out the entire threat. His daughter and the crew she's building needs to disappear."

"That's twenty-three bodies."

"We've hit compounds with more."

"We?"

"Us, Trenton, we've arranged a little party. You know Trenton doesn't take prisoners."

"We can't make that many disappear without bringing down heat. One person, me, I go in, I take as many as I can."

"Pure, you're not sacrificing yourself for him. What would Jenn say?"

"We talked about it, worst case scenario I go down and she makes sure Raul will always see a friendly face."

"Your Daddy wouldn't want that."

"My Daddy…" He let out a bitter laugh. "I saw the shot coming in the woods. I drew fire."

"Pure."

"I distracted the last shooter knowing he'd take me because I was in the open. Horace and Freddie were ordered to stay on Raul at all costs. I planned the entire operation. Raul was supposed to run when I was lifted out."

"Raul has never left you behind. How many operations was he on your Six? How many times did he refuse solo jobs because he wouldn't leave one of us to protect you? We have to end this. We destroy the Corzas, make an example."

"The only way to do that is to sever the head of the beast and clear Raul. How do we do that with minimal body count?" He preferred his plan, taking out the targets would put a definite end to the problem.

"The FBI wants Corza's head on a platter. No way do they want that bastard back on the streets, but they also want to neutralize her."

He made them a cup of coffee, and his plan shifted. He handed Gage a mug of black coffee.

"She wants to take over the city. The other bosses don't want that to happen. My sources tell me that she's too well protected. She throwing a welcome home party tomorrow night. She's invited all the heads of the families. I'd planned to find the best spot to start taking them out."

"Do you have ears in the house?"

"No, I got eyes on the outside." He pointed to his laptop on the table.

"You definitely did your homework."

He watched Gage scan the photos and timelines that filled one wall of the kitchen. Gage opened his laptop and logged in.

"Two weeks of surveillance."

"What has it showed you?"

"She wants to make an impression, and with the party, all the major players will be in house. If it was me, no one would be allowed inside with weapons, but she wants to build trust. She's going to try her charms, offer a partnership. We could make a few select kill shots and let them all take each other out in the chaos."

"Your talents are wasted as a sniper."

He rolled his eyes and sipped at his coffee.

"What else, Pure?"

"Cops would see it as a gang war, fight for supremacy gone terribly wrong. She'd be taken out in the firefight and Corza is obsessed with her. He's fighting so hard to get out to get back to her. I think she takes out the heads, then when her daddy comes home, he finds himself in an unmarked grave."

"You have to trust us, Pure, together we can get Raul out."

"Gage, I'll take the kill shot, don't y'all fuck me over." He turned away to start searching through his fridge for something to eat so he could take something for his ribs. Trusting them wasn't sitting well with him, but he had to put Raul's safety first. Taking her out was worth a few casualties, but as a thank you to Nero, he'd pass on the plan. Keeping Benito's former employer happy would keep Raul alive inside if it turned out his Daddy still had to serve a bit of time.

LITTLE AND LIV WERE POSTED DOWN THE BLOCK WITH EYES ON THE attendees. Horace and Freddie were tucked into a narrow alleyway ready to take out anyone who exited the back. He was positioned on the roof across the street. Gage and Linus were acting as bodyguards for Lawton, Nero's boss. It kept them close to the action to make sure the operation went as planned.

Hunter was back at the apartment and patched into Public Safety to assist in the getaway. He'd make sure it was green all the way to the docks. A panel truck waited for them to drive into and make it to a room they rented at a long-term hotel where the clerks didn't ask questions.

"Team two, you got eyes?" Linus' voice came through his earpiece.

"Yes. Full house." He braced his weapon and focused through the opened curtains. Everyone was playing nice. Through the mics they'd planted during the party setup, He could hear laughter and conversations, but it would be clearer once everyone sat down to discuss business over dinner.

"Pure," Peaches said his name.

"I have to focus."

"Look alive." He caught Gage tapping the earpiece to broadcast to the team. *"See y'all on the other side."*

Everyone fell into radio silence until Linus called for the breach. He scanned the interior as he watched everyone slowly make their way to the formal dining room. Only the bosses were allowed inside with one trusted man. The rest posted inside, as soon as shots were fired, everyone would converge to protect their bosses. He'd cover Lawton and Nero to make sure they got out.

Feedback signaled they'd lost ears.

"She jammed the signal."

He studied body language. Corza exuded confidence that far exceeded her years. The calm with which she carried herself eased the nerves of the bosses inside. She lulled them into a false sense of security. She was all business. Either they were thinking with their bank accounts and happy with a lucrative deal or they were thinking with their dicks? If he hadn't known what the meeting was about, he'd think it was all friends sharing a meal.

He started to relax, evened his breathing, and kept his entire focus on her. It was a change so subtle no one else wouldn't notice it. Her gaze went cold. As if in slow motion, she turned to look at each guard that posted themselves behind her chair.

"Peaches, get to the van."

Luckily, she didn't argue, and the weapons were drawn in all directions. It would take one shot. Chaos and paranoia. He had to focus on her. Gage and Linus had Nero covered. It's her smile that gave it away, muzzle fire and another player went down. He squeezed the trigger, the glass barely cracked, as he took out both her main guards.

He covered Gage and Linus as they extracted friendlies and then he followed the ascent of her arm, weapon drawn. He synced his shots with hers, one to each shoulder and she fired wildly. As he surged to his feet, he saw a hole open in the center of her forehead. They were on the move.

He glanced over the edge, dropped his weapon into the waiting arms of Freddie or Horace, the masks concealed which. His steps sounded too loud as he clipped the line into his carabiner and dove in a controlled descent to the street below. He stripped off his mask and gloves as he jogged down the alley. The van pulled to a stop with the side door open, and he jumped inside.

Adrenaline raced through his veins as the scream of sirens drew nearer, and they headed in the opposite direction. Minutes passed in slow motion as they took as many alleys as possible, then tires squealed.

"Guys, it's gonna be tight, speed up, you have ten seconds to make the next light and thirty before you converge with two marked. Keep it tight, and stash your gear now." Hunter's voice ordered, they stripped down to their tactical gear, exposed their bail enforcement vests and badges. Everything else was shoved into the secret compartment. Nero and Lawton were secured with flex-cuffs.

Little made the light, but he slowed and stopped to allow the cruisers to pass by. Everyone in the van held their breath until they were clear.

"You're running behind. Everyone is waiting, ramp is down. Drive in, and you'll head east. See you in twenty." Communication was cut, and Hunter would already be en route to the meet up at the hotel. Horace and Freddie were in charge of making the truck and van disappear.

"Did she go down?" Peaches asked.

"Yeah, but none of us took the kill shot," Gage answered from the back where he had eyes out the back window.

All light dimmed as they hit the ramp too quickly.

"Dammit, Little," Linus growled.

"Hunter said we were behind schedule."

The arguments raged around him, and he slid to Nero and Lawton. "Wrists." He cut the cuffs now that they were in the clear. Nero and Lawton would take a trip south until the heat died down. The survivors wouldn't be able to say anything more than Lawton's men extracted him when guns were drawn.

"If you ever want to make better money, give me a call," Lawton offered.

"I am in need of a job."

"The fuck you are. You don't need a new job until I fire your ass," Linus yelled. "Ally or not, Lawton, I'll take you down if you try to poach my people."

They settled in for the short ride to the hotel where they'd lie low for the night and go their separate ways the next morning. The high started to ease, and his ribs started to ache, and he needed a beer. But he wanted to see Raul, hear his voice, but he knew he wouldn't be in on the operation the next day. Gage and Linus would accompany Peaches to the prison. He wouldn't relax until he knew it was over, that Raul was safe and hopefully coming home.

NOTHING WAS AS IT SEEMED

*B*enito and he kept their backs to each other. They'd been ordered out of their cells and shackled in the middle of the night. Five officers had led them down to the lower-level of the facility. The air was humid from the exhaust system and musky—moldy air. They moved in perfect sync as they circled. The restraints had them at a disadvantage, but that didn't mean they wouldn't be able to cause damage in hand to hand combat.

"Who we piss off?"

"I got no idea. Maybe our friend wants a little retribution."

"Gentleman, sorry to wake you up so rudely."

"Fuck," they cursed in unison as the warden came out of the shadows into the open space.

"You two have some…influential friends."

"I'll take him and you—"

The man cut off Benito's plan. "Violence is unnecessary."

"C.O.s dragging inmates from bed in the middle of the night makes us less likely to be courteous."

"I see prison hasn't improved your attitude problems."

Peaches stepped up to stand beside the warden. Her suit was perfectly tailored, and if he wasn't mistaken, that was designer.

"Peaches, what are you doing here?"

"Peaches, as beautiful as I remember. You leave Gib yet? You know that man can't handle a woman like you."

"Benito," he said through gritted teeth.

"I've imagined the marks she could leave for twenty-five years."

"Behave, Benito, I have some good news for you later." Her heels echoed through the cavernous space until she stopped in front of them.

"Where's Pure?"

"Safe. He never hesitates to take the shot."

Relief went through him. For a minute, he'd thought she was there to inform him that Pure had started a war and hadn't made it out. "My boy is the best."

"For the reason we're here, we thought it was time you met the man who has been causing so many issues."

He caught movement from the corner of his eye, and Jenn appeared. She was outfitted in a vest, jeans, and a t-shirt. A bail enforcement badge around her neck. He was sure Pure hadn't approved of his mother being used on an operation. "Shit, what is—"

"I needed some assistance. Now, meet Anthony Corza."

Peaches pivoted to the side, and a man in cuffs and shackles stumbled into sight. The man wore a jumpsuit with inmate emblazoned across his chest. Corza had to be in his sixties but was still powerfully built. His dark eyes burned with hatred.

"What the fuck is going on?" Corza demanded.

"I'm glad you ask," Peaches said as she made a show of opening a file folder that she plucked from the warden's hands. "Warner, prepare."

He shot his gaze to Jenn, and she began to fill a syringe from a small bottle.

"You've caused me some significant issues. You messed with my boys, and I've been waiting for months to destroy you."

The coldness in Peaches' voice froze him through. The warden and a few officers flanked him, while three more kept shotguns trained on Corza. Peaches started dropping photos onto the ground at Corza's feet. As she did, she named crime bosses, ten in total, and he felt Benito tense as the former boss' name was called. Yet, he ignored that as the smirk on Corza's mouth pulled into a sadistic smirk.

"Oh, I forgot one."

Everything changed when the soft whisper of paper hit the floor, and Corza lost his mind. He started to fight forward when Jenn entered the danger zone, but all fighting ceased when the needle pushed into the side of Corza's thick neck. The man had transitioned from pride to devastation to anger in seconds, then the mysterious needle.

"She was a very beautiful girl, but..." Peaches paused and pulled out her phone.

"Daddy served his purpose. You stick to the plan. As soon as he steps foot outside, you better take the fucking shot, or you'll be buried next to him."

"A daughter to make a man proud. She wanted to be queen and to do that everyone knows the king has to be sacrificed."

"What the fuck do you want?"

"Your organization is done. You're all that's left. But if you don't call off your dogs, then my colleague here has a lethal dose of an untraceable paralytic. You'll suffocate to death. And let me tell you, her son got caught in the crossfire of your men trying to take Raul out. She's been waiting for a bit of revenge."

"I'm quite familiar with how to make a death look... accidental. Although, I'd like you to suffer."

"Warner."

He knew Peaches too well, she was amused, and he had to admit he was a little proud of the adorable woman.

"Corza, what you're going to do is admit to your crimes and make your way back to the hole they buried you in a decade ago. If my son's name even makes it into your thoughts, I'm going to let Warner take her revenge."

Son. He caught Peaches' gaze when she looked over her shoulder at him.

"What's your answer? And just to help you along, everyone knows that you ordered the takedown of most of their bosses. The warden has assured me he'll make sure you get a nice warm welcome in general population."

He tried to rush forward when the man spit at Peaches, but before he could make it to her, Corza's head snapped back as Peaches' fist connected with his jaw and Jenn held up an empty syringe.

"You bitch," Corza screamed and tried to get to Jenn.

"Oh, sorry, I picked up the wrong vial, saline isn't lethal. My mistake."

"Warden, return him to the transport van."

"Very well, Mrs. Phelps. If I never see you again, my heart won't break."

"Same to you."

He saw everyone leave until just him, Benito, and Peaches and Jenn were left. And a few officers. He returned to Benito's side, and they frowned at each other when their restraints were removed.

"Officers, you can leave us alone now," Peaches ordered like she owned the place. Hell, she could.

"Raul, you're going to plead guilty to the escape, assault of the officers, and destruction of government property, you will be sentenced to a year, you'll serve four months."

"I can deal with that. What's Benito get?"

"Gentlemen," Peaches voice echoed. "Benito, meet Agents Scanlon and Drew, on the day Raul walks out of here, you do as well. I have explained that you were instrumental in providing the intel to take down the Corza family and saving several undercover agents in the process."

"I'm not a rat, Peaches."

"You're not. This is completely off the record. I have a friend who occasionally makes some lucrative deals for inmates with potential. These Agents who you've never met will inform everyone in law enforcement that you died while incarcerated. And best thing, you get to do something you're good at."

"I knew my skills would pay off. What do I owe you, Peaches?"

"Nothing. You took care of Raul, and we both know you didn't owe me anything. I didn't get that not guilty."

"You know I was never going to get away clean. And you gotta admit you made my stay here a lot more comfortable. Will I be locked up waiting for this secret person to need me?"

"Nope, you're free to move around, but you will have a handler that will make sure you don't take up your old hobby."

Benito chuckled, and he said goodbye as he was led away by the agents and he was left with Peaches and Jenn.

"Is Pure okay?"

"Yes, the operation went well. The team showed up before he could do something stupid," Peaches said. "I'm going to leave you with Jenn. I'll be by tomorrow, and we're meeting with the District Attorney to go over your deal. You know this has to be done."

"Yeah, he's covered my ass more than I deserve, and I'd serve life if it kept him safe."

"You and Pure pull this type of shit again, and I'll have some old friends hide your bodies. I know we didn't back you up, but that didn't mean we didn't think you were innocent. We were working with what we had, and there's only so many strings we could pull. This had to be on the up and up. Pure was a perfectly rational son until you came along."

He nodded and listened to Peaches' heels click then disappear as a heavy, metal door slammed in the distance.

"How is he really?"

He leaned into her sudden hug, and she buried her face against his chest. He held her tightly as he waited for them both to process. He was walking out of here alive and back to his boy. That was all he'd wanted.

"He's good. He's at the apartment and will be until you come home."

"What about work?"

"He's taking an extended leave until you're free. He refuses to work with anyone but you. Also, there's some fences in need of mending between him and the Crew."

"I'm sorry, Jenn."

"Son, don't you apologize to me. You're family. Also, I didn't make the best impression on your parents when I went to visit them. Let's just say they're not going to come to the wedding."

For the first time in months, he laughed loudly and squeezed her again. "I think I'd already figured that out."

"Their loss became my gain."

"You look good in that bail enforcement gear."

He snorted as she went all supermodel as she showed off and did a perfect pivot.

"Thank you, should I put in an application?"

"No, you were having way too much fun tonight."

He turned his head as an officer came up to them.

"Martinez, we gotta get you back before the next shift starts doing bed checks."

"Four months and you'll be home, just keep it together until then."

"I promise, keep him sane until I get home."

"Always."

He let them put his restraints back on, and he quietly made his way back to his cell. Once inside, he laid down on his bunk and stared up at the wire support of the top bunk. He'd started to give in to the fact he was in here for life or until Corza came to take him out, but he saw the end in sight. He'd be home with his boy, and he wouldn't take another day for granted. All he had to do was keep his head down until he walked out of the gate to his boy. Pure would be there waiting, there like he'd always been for him.

THIS WAS THE HAPPILY EVER AFTER

*H*e lifted onto the tailgate of his new truck and waited outside the gates for his Daddy to walk out. Months of nothing more than weekly visits and phone calls, and he wanted his Daddy home where he belonged. The murder charges were dropped, but unfortunately, they wanted to teach Raul a lesson and made him serve time for the escape. They hadn't touched in nearly four months. They'd ushered Raul away at the sentencing where he'd pled guilty for escape and destruction of government property for the van.

He hopped down to the ground and smiled at the man beyond the chain-link fence. He shoved his hands into his back pockets and crossed the parking lot just as the gate opened. His Daddy had packed on another thirty pounds of muscle, his goatee touched his chest, and his wavy hair was long enough to tangle around his fingers.

Raul opened his arms, and he ran into them. His Daddy's lips took his almost brutally as he was walked backward to the truck. He whimpered as Raul grabbed his ass. The hold shifted the plug he'd inserted after he'd prepared himself for Daddy's homecoming.

"You better have a room nearby."

"I see how it is. Daddy just missed his boy's body."

"It's all your fault and those naughty encoded messages."

"Nice touch, huh," he whispered, and his face hurt from smiling. He inhaled the scent of Raul. Absorbed his Daddy's warmth. His Daddy's hard dick digging into his soft stomach wasn't bad either. "We're about ten minutes from the room I rented before we drive home." He hugged Raul's neck tight as he was manhandled into the passenger seat and he froze as his Daddy rubbed his denim-covered dick.

He laughed as his Daddy growled and slammed the door, Raul was running around and hopping into the driver's seat. The tires spun, and gravel pinged against nearby vehicles.

"Impatient?"

"I've spent four months away from you. Seeing you through fucking glass. Daddy's patience disappeared a long time ago, baby boy."

He gave Raul directions and his face heated at the looks his Daddy kept giving him. He wasn't any better. And he had a surprise for his Daddy when they got to their motel room.

"Have you been playing with yourself while Daddy's been away?"

"Yes, Daddy."

"Daddy has been keeping track of your punishment, and it's time you learned your lesson. Daddy's good boy doesn't touch himself when I can't watch."

"Is that, right?" he asked. He worked his belt loose, popped the button on his jeans, and lowered his zipper. He slipped his hand into the opening of the denim and pulled out his hard cock. "A mile ahead on the right." His voice broke as he slowly stroked his cock from base to tip, then back down.

"You getting ready to fuck Daddy?"

"Room twenty-six on the backside." He kept stroking, making the fat head slick with pre-cum.

When Raul pulled to a stop in front of their room, he leaned over the console. "Your boy is wearing a plug."

"Get in the room and strip...now."

He shivered at the hard edge to his Daddy's order and he half-assed tucked himself in. He was practically running for the door, had it unlocked and inside, and he spun to walk backward to keep his gaze on his Daddy. For months, he'd found himself, took charge of his pleasure, and experimented with playing with his hole. At first, he'd hesitated, waiting for the memories because he didn't have his Daddy to focus on.

The door clicked shut with a scarily quiet click, and he lifted his arms to grab the cotton of his t-shirt to pull it over his head.

"S'fucking beautiful, dreamed of you every night. Only to wake up reaching out to pull you close. I missed you so much, baby boy."

"I missed you too, Daddy." He kicked off his sneakers and his bare feet sunk into the carpet. He pushed his jeans down his hips to expose his superhero underwear.

"Did you like playing with your hole?"

"Not at first, I was too nervous, and the toy wasn't you."

"No toy will ever live up to your Daddy."

"Are you getting naked, Daddy?"

He stood there nervously in his underwear as he watched his Daddy strip. Raul's dick hard and the foreskin still covering the smooth head. He could still taste his Daddy—his tongue remembering the texture of loose skin and silky cockhead. He clocked his Daddy's every move as Raul strolled to the bed and laid down.

"Come here, baby boy, but first take off the cute underwear."

"Yes, Daddy."

He removed them quickly and rushed to the bed to lie down.

"Lie on your back, pull your legs back, and show Daddy your toy."

He did as he was commanded without hesitation. His body

belonged to Daddy—everything he was would always be Raul's. He'd known it even as his fear masked it.

"There's never been a happier Daddy than me. My boy makes me so proud. Strong and self-reliant, vulnerable but so confident. Daddy has loved you for so long."

His lips trembled under the press of Raul's and his chest tightened. "Nicolas Warner, I love you."

He gasped because it was the first time they'd said it out loud. They sent it in messages or said what they loved about each other, but had silently agreed to not say it to each other until they were able to touch and kiss.

"I love you too, Raul."

No more words were shared as they kissed and caressed, sweat drenched their skin, and their breathing turned harsh. His Daddy fucked him slowly with the plug, making sure he was nice and stretched for him. He arched his neck at the sharp suction as Raul began to leave marks from his collarbone as he moved lower. He looked down the length of his body to his Daddy's loving gaze on his face.

His body seized as his Daddy swallowed his cock and roughly tortured him until he was fighting to push Daddy away. He jerked with every pulse around the head of his dick.

"Daddy, Daddy, stop—"

As soon as the first syllable of the last word passed his lips, Raul backed off, and rough hands took hold of his face. His Daddy had issued him a safeword, but the painful pleasure had been too much.

"Too much, Daddy."

"And Daddy will always stop. Nicolas, stop, no, or anything else will always make me stop. Your consent is the sexiest thing about loving on you."

He was embarrassed by the tears leaking from the corners of his eyes. The plug eased from his hole and then Raul was sitting back on his heels. Raul rolled a condom onto his fat cock.

Daddy made sure to lube his cock and slicked his hole inside and out.

"May Daddy love on you?"

"Yes, Daddy."

He felt every inch as his Daddy's thickness split his hole wide.

"Oh, fuck, Daddy." He groaned as his Daddy's hips met his ass.

A smack to his thigh made him freeze.

"Baby boy, Daddy doesn't like those bad words from his good boy's mouth."

"Sorry, Daddy."

His felt his brow furrow and his teeth cut into his bottom lip as Daddy retreated, and slammed forward pushing another fuck past his lips. The more he cussed, the harder his Daddy fucked his hole—owned it. His Daddy tortured him repeatedly as he continuously changed from slow to fast, gentle to brutal. He was clawing at the comforter, twisted his body and arching until he curled his hips, holding still as he looked down to watch his Daddy's cock working his ass.

He grabbed his cock and jacked off.

"Daddy, I'm gonna...Daddy!" His voice broke, and he grabbed his Daddy behind his neck and pulled Raul's mouth to his and his release spread between their bellies.

"Goddammit, baby boy, milk Daddy's cock."

His Daddy took him in quick, shallow thrusts and then his Daddy froze. The sharp edges of his Daddy's teeth pinched his lip as his Daddy's hips ground against his ass, then they both collapsed, and Raul's fingers fisted in his hair as the kiss they shared roughened.

"You'll always be mine. Daddy's the only one to make his boy's dreams come true."

"Move in with me, Daddy."

"Try to get rid of me."

He chuckled as his Daddy eased from him. Then he watched as his Daddy removed the condom and tied it off to toss it in the basket beside the bed. He was pulled into his Daddy's strong arms. He nuzzled his Daddy's chest and then tipped his head to kiss the stubble covered skin beneath Raul's chin.

"Thank you for waiting for me, Nicolas."

"Always."

They cuddled and talked, planned their future. Shared dreams and secrets. This is what Pure had wanted, the person his mother had told him to wait for and one night of violence hadn't taken his happiness. It hadn't broken him as he'd thought. It had taught him that he could love past the pain. He could demand the love he deserved. This was the happily ever after.

EPILOGUE

THIS SOUNDED EASIER IN THE BOOKS

"*C*ome on, baby boy, wake up," he whispered in Pure's ear as he tried to wake his boy up. Lack of sleep was becoming the normal for them, but they weren't getting a lot of couple-time lately.

"The babies are asleep, shut up, Daddy, and go back—"

He bit the side of Pure's neck. "Daddy got you all nice and ready." He played with the base of the plug he'd inserted after his boy's bath last night. As much as he loved when his boy fucked him, there was nothing like the trust and submission when Pure gave in to him.

He shifted his boy onto his knees, his ass in the air and his face buried in the pillow.

"Daddy?"

"Yes, boy?" He gripped the base of the plug, fucking his boy's stretched hole. In the two years since they'd made promises in private—their own vows—he still desperately needed his boy. They never skipped an opportunity to say I love you or show they cared.

Pure didn't say a word as his hips lifted. He groaned as his boy grabbed his hairy cheeks and pulled them apart. All his control fled as he jerked the toy from his boy's ass and positioned himself behind Pure. He sloppily slicked his cock, held the base, and slammed forward.

"Daddy," Pure muffled his scream in the pillow.

He forced his boy to take every inch at his pace. Pure gripped as his hair and bit into his bicep.

"Boy, you don't hide from Daddy." He spanked Pure in punishment for hiding his pleasure from him. He reamed Pure's tight hole until they fought for dominance. Pure pushing back and him slamming forward, their bodies connecting with loud slapping of sweat-drenched skin. He spanked Pure harder, and Pure contracted around his cock to the point of pain.

He blanketed his boy's back, pressed his lips to his ear. He fisted his fingers in Pure's hair and jerked his boy's head back.

"You don't take unless Daddy gives you permission, baby boy." He deep stroked at a brutal pace. "Daddy should leave you unsatisfied."

Pure desperately clawed at his hips as he began to retreat.

"No, Daddy, I'll be good, I promise. Just fuck me, Daddy."

"Good boys don't say such nasty things." He slammed his hand over Pure's mouth and fucked his ass cruelly. He'd learned his boy liked to be fucked. Held down and taken, all on his terms —his choice—a reclaiming of his power. His baby boy's screams muffled and then Pure was grabbing onto the headboard until his knuckles turned white. Pure's body arched violently and bore down on his cock. He spilled his release as he sealed his hips to his boy's ass.

They both collapsed on the bed, fighting for breath, and he kept shallowly stroking to draw out their pleasure. Their privacy was limited, but he always took the time to soothe his boy after an intense orgasm. He kissed his boy's lazy smile and savored the stroke of Pure's fingers through his shaggy, wavy hair.

He growled as two excited voices and a third pissed off grumbling came over the baby monitor. He swore their son was cussing out his sisters' in baby talk.

"I'll go take care of them while you clean up." He rose to his knees, easing out of his boy's red, swollen hole. He placed a kiss between Pure's shoulder blades then quickly got dressed to get to the bathroom to wash his hands and then off to the nursery.

THE TWO TINY GIRLS WERE ON EITHER SIDE OF THEIR BROTHER, hugging him for all he was worth and Desi was having a meltdown. First thing in the morning affection from his sisters wasn't his favorite thing. He required a bit more waking up than his balls-to-the-walls sisters.

"Give me Desi," Pure demanded and picked him up, carrying him out of the room to get their bottles ready.

"Princesses, you have to stop torturing your brother," he said as he smiled at his and Pure's daughters. They had his dark hair and deep tan skin, while Desi was all Pure. They'd had two embryos implanted, Nicole and Billie came from one, and Desi the other. They'd left it to chance and received three surprises. He'd never expected to fall in love at first sight with three very tiny pissed off humans.

They'd been so small, and over a month early. The first month, while they had to stay in the hospital, had been filled with sleepless nights and worry. Pure's soft cries awakening Raul as he worried about their children's future. The joy of their birth exploded into fear as Desi fought to breathe that first twenty-four hours.

He quickly changed them and picked them up to go join Pure in the kitchen. He stopped in the doorway and remembered another morning with a kitchen filled with kids. His boy making breakfast. It didn't seem like two years had passed or that he would've come to be the one to make his boy's dreams come true.

This is the dream he'd had as he'd spent months in prison, waiting for his release day to set him free. Those first days of worry, not knowing if his boy had survived. The missed opportunity to tell his boy he'd loved him.

They had learned their lesson. They didn't wait for the right time to do or say what was needed; even if that ended in the start of a fight. They'd allowed too much to fester, had made mistakes, but no longer. He approached Pure with their daughters hugging his neck in a chokehold far stronger than their size.

He stopped in front of his boy and leaned in, brushing his mouth over Pure's. "You forgot to tell me something, didn't you, baby boy?"

He took in the sweet tilt of Pure's lips. "I love you, Daddy."

"Good boy, I love you too."

They wrapped their arms around each other, their son squeaking as he made himself heavy in an attempt to escape the group hug. His perfect boy, their overly dramatic son, and two highly affectionate daughters were the future he hadn't seen coming, but he'd never take it for granted.

He groaned as they separated. They had an hour and a half to feed the babies and get breakfast themselves before Princess showed up to watch the triplets. Then him and Pure were off to work. Things at Trenton had slowly worked out. Everyone agreed mistakes were made. They loved their jobs, but life had changed. Pure and him alternated jobs. Only working together when a full team was needed. They wanted to make sure one of them was always home at night with their daughters and son. Family was always the most important thing for them— everything else came second.

He also accepted something else since his prison stay. Family wasn't about the blood that ran through their veins or the name shared. It was about acceptance and care, the people who always had their backs. Forgiveness for missteps. Before Powers and the Crews, he would've never seen this life for himself. Yet, even if he'd taken a different path, some part of him knew that it would be like a missing piece—a regret for some unknown thing. But he didn't have to worry about that. This was the happily ever after they deserved and suffered to attain.

ABOUT THE AUTHOR

J.M. Dabney is a multi-genre author who writes Body Positive/Diverse Romance and Fiction. They live with a constant diverse cast of characters in their head. No matter their size, shape, race, etc. J.M. lives for one purpose alone, and that's to make sure they do them justice and give them the happily ever after they deserve. J.M. is dysfunction at its finest and they makes sure their characters are a beautiful kaleidoscope of crazy. There is nothing more they want from telling their stories than to show that no matter the package the characters come in or the damage their pasts have done, that love is love. That normal is never normal and sometimes the so-called broken can still be amazing.

The author is Gender Nonconforming are uses the preferred pronouns They/Them.

ALSO BY J.M. DABNEY

Sappho's Kiss Series

When All Else Fails

More Than What They See

Dysfunction it its Finest Series

Club Revenge

Soul Collector Prophecy

Twirled World Ink Series

Berzerker

Trouble

Scary

Lucky

Brawlers Series

Crave

Psycho

Bull

Hunter

Executioners Series

Ghost

Joker

King

Sin & Saint

Trenton Security

Livingston

Little

Gage

Pure

Masiello Brothers

The Taming of Violet

3 Moments Trilogy

A Matter of Time

The Men of Canter Handyman

Black Leather & Knuckle Tattoos

Chance at the Impossible

Bloody Knuckles Bar & Grill

Clipping the Gargoyle's Wings

New West City Universe

Co-written with Davidson King

The Hunt

Standalone

By Way of Pain (Criminal Delights - Assassins)

Waited So Long